To John —
all best wishes!

Stonewall Jackson at Gettysburg

Douglas Lee Gibboney

22. Dec. 10

And men will tell their children
Tho' all other memories fade
How they fought with Stonewall Jackson
In the old Stonewall Brigade.

(John Esten Cooke, 1863, "The Song of the Rebel")

D1558916

BURD STREET PRESS
SHIPPENSBURG, PENNSYLVANIA

Copyright © 2002 by Douglas Lee Gibboney

ALL RIGHTS RESERVED—No part of this book may be reproduced in any form
without permission in writing from the publisher, except by a reviewer who wishes to quote
brief passages in connection with a review.

This Burd Street Press publication
was printed by
Beidel Printing House, Inc.
63 West Burd Street
Shippensburg, PA 17257-0708 USA

The acid-free paper used in this book meets the guidelines for permanence and
durability of the Committee on Production Guidelines for Book Longevity of the Council on
Library Resources.

First Printing, 1996, Second Printing, 1997
Third Printing, 2002

First & Second Printing by
Sergeant Kirkland's Museum and Historical Society, Inc.
Fredericksburg, Virginia

Third Printing by
Burd Street Press, Division of White Mane Publishing Co., Inc.
Shippensburg, Pennsylvania

For a complete list of available publications
please write
Burd Street Press
Division of White Mane Publishing Company, Inc.
P.O. Box 708
Shippensburg, PA 17257-0708 USA

ISBN 1-57249-317-8 (formerly ISBN 1-887901-04-3 - formerly Library of Congress
Catalog Number 96-6956)

Library of Congress Cataloging-in-Publication Data

Gibboney, Douglas Lee, 1953-
    Stonewall Jackson at Gettysburg / Douglas Lee Gibboney.
    p. cm.
    Summary: In this fictional memoir which assumes that Stonewall Jackson survived his
wounding at Chancellorsville in May of 1863, young Jefferson Carter Randolph
describes his wartime experiences with the General at the Battle of Gettysburg and in the
months that followed.
    Includes bibliographical references.
    ISBN 1-57249-317-8 (alk. paper)
    1. Jackson, Stonewall, 1824-1863--Fiction. 2. Gettysburg, Battle of, Gettysburg, Pa.,
1863--Fiction. 3. United States--History--Civil War, 1861-1865--Fiction. [1. Gettysburg,
Battle of, Gettysburg, Pa., 1863--Fiction. 2. Jackson, Stonewall, 1824-1863--Fiction. 3.
Confederate States of America--Army--Fiction. 4. United States--History--Civil War,
1861-1865--Campaigns--Fiction.] I. Title.

PS3557.I1391686 S76 2002
[Fic]--dc20
                                                                              2002071664

PRINTED IN THE UNITED STATES OF AMERICA

To Carolyn

TABLE OF CONTENTS

ACKNOWLEDGMENTS

No book can be successfully completed without support and assistance. Special thanks are due to the following people who helped in the preparation of this work: William C. Davis, Mechanicsburg, Pennsylvania; Scott and Eileen Dray, Rogers, Ohio; Anne Gunshenan, Palmyra, Pennsylvania; and, especially, Ronald R. Seagrave, Director, Sergeant Kirkland's Museum and Historical Society, Fredericksburg, Virginia, who made this text a reality; and to his assistant, Mary Lou Cramer, who helped proof this writer's work. A special note of appreciation should go to Dr. Pia S. Seagrave, the editor of the second edition. My thanks also go to White Mane Publishing for bringing out this new edition.

Civil War Fiction for People ...

Who Don't Read Civil War Fiction!

Over the past thirty-plus years, I have spent many idle hours reading hundreds of true accounts of America's bloodiest war. This volume, however, has its roots in fiction published around the time of the Civil War Centennial: MacKinley Kantor's *If the South Had Won the Civil War* and the series of John Mosby novels written by Ray Hogan. It is also kin to Robert Fowler's *Jim Mundy*, another fictional memoir.

With the exception of the narrator and his family, all named persons and places mentioned did exist and, with the obvious exception of Stonewall Jackson, were present during what did and what could have occurred.

In recent years, serious Civil War scholarship has reached impressive levels but this is your invitation to suspend disbelief and go on an idle daydream as history slips a cog.

Douglas Lee Gibboney

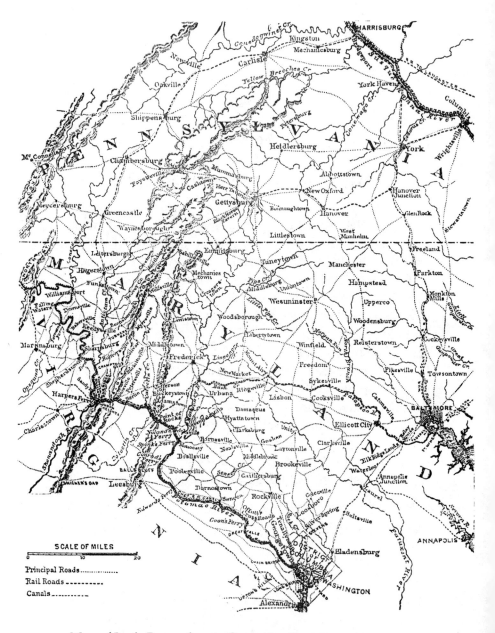

Map of Lee's Pennsylvania Campaign (Battles and Leaders)

Chapter One

HOW I JOINED THE ARMY

My name is Jefferson Carter Randolph and I was born July 7, 1847, in the small town of Lexington, Virginia. My father was James Monroe Randolph and my mother was Sarah Mosby Carter. On each side, my family claimed distinguished lineage; my mother believed herself a descendant of "King" Carter while my father boasted of distant kinship with the squire of Monticello. However, in my twilight years, I have undertaken a study of this and have been unable to prove any of it.

My childhood passed happily in Lexington. Father ran several small, but successful, businesses and we also enjoyed a steady income off investments inherited from Grandfather Carter. We had a comfortable home near Washington College as well as a small working farm outside town.

Our family included three slaves. Robert and Thelma tended the farm while Sally, who had been with my mother nearly all her life, carried on as our cook.

In my youth, I gave little thought to the system of slavery, assuming that was just the natural order of things. I also assumed that all slaves were treated as well as those our family owned. Like most Virginians, when the war came, I fought to protect my native state from invasion. The question of slavery should have been resolved without fighting but hot-headed politicians on both sides exploited the issue for their own purposes and the result can be seen in cemeteries throughout the country. Given the hindsight of old age, I can only say that the South is better off now than it was when our "peculiar institution" existed.

Our farm was not far from the one owned by Thomas Jonathan Jackson, then a professor at the Virginia Military Institute and soon to become the famous "Stonewall." Major Jackson, as he was known, enjoyed the respect of the community, both for his position at the military academy and for his activity in the Presbyterian Church, where he was an elder. He and my father belonged to the debating society and he occasionally visited our home. Still, few would have ventured that Major Jackson would become such a renowned son of Mars when the war began.

To be quite candid, Major Jackson did not cut an impressive figure, particularly in civilian dress. Of average weight and height, he had a high forehead and a bristly beard. He would have passed unnoticed in a crowd unless one of his unusual habits drew attention. For example, my father saw him walking one day with an arm extended in the air to "even out the blood flow and restore the balance."

I recall vividly one episode just prior to the war. It came in early spring, during the crisis at Fort Sumter but before shots were fired. Major Jackson and my father were having an involved discussion on the porch of his house and my father indicated his opposition to secession.

Jackson's head sank to his chest in thought for a moment; then he turned to my father and fixed his gaze upon him. "But if it comes, sir, we shall do our duty," he said. "We must do our duty."

Like many Virginians, my father continued to oppose secession until Lincoln's call went out for volunteers to suppress the rebellion. When the state voted to leave the union, my father left, too. Within days, both he and Jackson were gone to the war.

How I longed to accompany them! The excitement of the marching soldiers, beating drums and colorful, unfurled flags was almost unbearable. But I was just thirteen and they would not take me.

My mother and I followed the war news avidly and read each of my father's letters countless times. He was stationed at Harper's Ferry, serving under Jackson, who had been advanced to brigadier general in June.

In late July came the distressing news that my father had been seriously wounded by a cannon shot at the great first battle of Manassas. Father's leg was amputated and he returned home to us a few weeks afterward. Though his body was not intact, his spirit was and he now became the most avid Rebel in Rockbridge County.

At Manassas, General Jackson rose to national prominence for his brigade's stand against the Yankee onslaught. From that time on, he was known as "Stonewall," although he always insisted that the honor belonged not to him but to the brigade.

We were particularly cheered when "Stonewall" was put in command of troops in the lower Shenandoah Valley. I yearned for the great general, whose visage I had once taken for granted, to return to Lexington for a visit. But it was nearly two years before General Jackson came back to us and then under sad circumstances.

Through 1862 and the first half of 1863, I continued my schooling and worked in the store with Father. I found it deadly dull. Who wants to sit in a shop all day when the fate of your nation is being decided on distant fields?

Much of my time was spent on my horse, riding the countryside and pretending to scout for Yankees. On one of these excursions, I found the body of one of our soldiers along the road. He, apparently, died while trying to return home. Someone had looted his effects and we could not identify him beyond the North Carolina buttons on his butternut jacket. At the time, I wondered what kind of ghoul could steal from a dead man but, before the war ended, my own boots had come off a Yankee corpse and I was glad to have them.

The wounding of Jackson at Chancellorsville.

As students of the war know, General Jackson received a serious wound on the night of May 2 during his successful attack on General Hooker's right flank at the Battle of Chancellorsville. Scouting between the lines, the General and several members of his staff, Captain J. K. Boswell, Captain R. F. Wilburne, Lieutenant Joseph G. Morrison, aide-de-camp, and five or six couriers were fired upon by our own men.[1] The General was shot in the hand and tossed heavily to the ground by his horse, "Little Sorrel." The fall caused some head injury. He was taken from the field and did not regain lucidity until the next day at the Wilderness Tavern.

Accompanied by Mrs. Jackson and their small daughter, the General went first to Richmond, Virginia, and then to Lexington to recover.[2] Though his arrival was meant to be a secret, it was a secret that could not be kept and a guard had to be posted on Washington Street to keep the curious away.

Through the early months of 1863, I renewed my campaign to persuade my parents to allow me to join the army. The victories at Fredericksburg and Chancellorsville convinced me that soon the war would end with a Southern victory. I was determined not to be left out of it. When General Jackson returned to Lexington, my sixteenth birthday was less than two months away.

My father received an ultimatum: either I be permitted to join the army or I would run away and do so, anyhow. Instead of whipping me for my insolence, he gave me a sorrowful look and said, "I shall see General Jackson and perhaps you can go with him."

My spirits soared. Not only would I be allowed to join the army but I might go with the man who, after perhaps General Lee, was our greatest commander.

My father gained an audience with "Stonewall" the following night. He dressed in his old uniform and used his

---

[1] Captain J. K. Boswell was killed instantly.

[2] Anna Jackson wanted her husband taken to North Carolina to recover at her family's home, but the General insisted upon Lexington.

crutch to hobble down the street. Gone for forty minutes, he returned and instructed me to go at once and see the General.

I approached the house with trepidation. My father had offered no clue as to the results of his interview and I lacked any understanding of what to expect.

I mounted the stairs and knocked. Mrs. Jackson greeted me warmly and I entered the drawing room to find General Jackson on the floor, playing with their baby girl.

Jackson wore civilian clothes, a coarse, striped shirt, dark pants, and carpet slippers. Except for the bandages on his head and hand, he looked little changed from the man I had known before the war. Silly youth that I was, this confused and disappointed me.

He smiled at my entrance and asked, "Sir, are you an early riser?"

This strange greeting startled me and I stammered, more or less truthfully, that I was.

"Good. That's good," he said, "I will only have gentlemen who are early risers on my staff."

We talked for twenty minutes. He asked many more questions and I answered them, though I cannot recall another specific of our conversation until the very end when he said, "Very good. I can use another courier now that Charlie Randolph's gone to the institute.[3] We leave for the army in three days. Go home and pack, but take only half of what you think you need."

"Yes, sir!" I saluted and rushed from the room, nearly knocking Mrs. Jackson over in my haste. I was to be a soldier on the staff of "Stonewall" Jackson.

---

[3] A distant cousin of Jefferson Randolph who served as Jackson's courier early in the war and was later wounded as a VMI cadet at the Battle of New Market, Virginia.

The only known photograph of Jefferson Carter Randolph was discovered at *The Picket Post*, Fredericksburg, Virginia, in 1996, nearly 133 years after it had been taken.

As I reached the door, the General called to me, "Tell no one except your ma and pa of our plans. I wish to depart without ceremony!"

My mother took these developments badly but she quickly set to work, making several shirts of heavy cotton flannel for me. She also tailored an old Virginia Military Institute uniform jacket which my father had obtained, along with a pair of red flannel pants that I found in the attic. These added, I thought, a stylish Zouave effect to my costume. When my father saw the pants, he forbade me to wear them, saying that I didn't need to give the Yankees anything bright to shoot at. He left and returned with some fine cadet gray wool which my mother made into trousers. At my urging, she sewed a gold stripe down the seam of each leg. A black slouch hat and riding boots completed my military appearance and I spent much time gazing at myself before the dressing mirror.

On the day I left, my mother cried and my father presented me with the Navy Colt revolver and holster he had worn at Manassas and the iron-mounted saber he had carried in the Mexican War. My mother remained home while my father used his crutch to escort me as far as the General's house. It was the last I saw of my parents; they both died of consumption while I was a prisoner of the Yankees.

My military ardor had been dampened by the pain of leave-taking, which I saw mirrored in General Jackson's own farewell. Other than the servants, I was the only one present as he tenderly kissed his wife and infant goodbye. He spoke a few quiet words to Mrs. Jackson in Spanish and I grew uncomfortable at being witness to such an intimate scene. But then Jackson turned, called abruptly for me to come along, and we exited onto the porch.

Despite Jackson's wishes, a crowd stood outside in the street to witness the hero's departure. They shouted for a speech but "Stonewall" demurred until he had settled into the saddle. Then he said, in a low voice, which only part of the crowd could hear, "This town holds all that is dear to me. If a merciful God will grant us a quick and victorious end to this war, I shall return and leave no more."

The two of us, along with Jackson's servant, Jim, rode to the packet landing with the crowd in tow. We took the canal boat to Lynchburg where another crowd awaited us. We worked our way through the well-wishers and boarded the cars for Richmond. I had anticipated the chance for substantial conversations with the General on the long journey. But it seemed that, even in the remotest parts of civilization, people gathered to cheer his passage. He suffered almost constant annoyance and interruption. I also realized that the General's injuries still bothered him and he tired quite easily. Much of the trip he spent sleeping.

He did devote some time to lecturing me on military ways and organization. During these lessons, his tone and manner assumed the somber and rather dull cadences of the professor that he had once been. I listened carefully, trying to absorb every morsel of information.

Jackson spoke highly of Napoleon and talked, in great detail, of a visit to the Waterloo battlefield during his European tour, before the war. He concluded this lecture with words that seemed to summarize his military genius.

"Randolph, a commander must always mystify, mislead and surprise the enemy. Unless absolutely necessary, he should never fight against heavy odds; instead, he should maneuver his troops to strike the weakest portion of the enemy's forces and crush it! By attacking in detail, a smaller army may destroy a larger one. That is the only way our outnumbered armies can hope to win our nation's independence."

Upon finally reaching the capital of the Confederacy at Richmond, yet another crowd awaited and there were, again, calls for a speech. Jackson merely waved and a guard of soldiers hustled us past, much to the throng's displeasure. The General booked into the Spottswood Hotel and went from there to pay his respects to President Jefferson Davis. No invitation to visit the President being extended to me, I continued along to my uncle's house on Broad Street.

The next day I rose early, met the General, and we traveled on the cars to the army near Fredericksburg. The General again slept most of the trip, though he awoke as we neared our destination and closely examined the military stores when we passed through Guiney's Station. For miles around the army's encampment, the countryside had a worn, beaten-down appearance and nearly all the trees had been cut for firewood.

I shall never forget our reception when the train reached the railhead near Hamilton Crossing. By then, I had become inflated with my own importance. After all, there I was, a boy of fifteen, and practically an intimate of General T. J. Jackson. As we departed the cars, a military band struck up "Dixie" and more soldiers than I had ever imagined began waving their caps and giving the wild Rebel yell. It looked like the entire Army of Northern Virginia, or at least its Second Corps, had gathered for our arrival. I followed the General toward a group of officers.

General Jackson spoke first to a distinguished man with a gray beard who wore a straw hat and had a dark linen duster over his uniform. General Jackson turned and introduced me to General Robert Edward Lee. I reached forward and shook his gloved hand. The mixture of pained and amused looks from the surrounding officers alerted me to my error and I quickly threw in an awkward salute for good measure.

Lee gave a smile. "It's all right. I can tell you will be a brave fellow and serve General Jackson well." With that remark, Robert E. Lee won, forever, my affection and loyalty.

Chapter Two

THE INVASION BEGINS

I had but little time to get used to my new surroundings. Jackson's return signaled that the army would soon embark on a new campaign. Shortly after our arrival, preparations were underway to break camp and the army was abuzz with rumors. Everyone believed we would be heading north for the decisive battle.

I rarely saw the General during that time, as he was closeted with Generals Lee and Longstreet. Alexander "Sandie" Pendleton, whom I knew from Lexington, took me under his wing and introduced me to the other members of the General's military family. Sandie served as the General's chief of staff and was one of the most popular men in the army. Throughout the campaign, he offered immeasurable kindness to me and, even today, I can scarcely think of him without weeping.

Two days after our arrival, a general order announced that General Richard S. Ewell would return to the army from convalescent leave and take command of the late General Ambrose Hill's "Light Division." Hill, a capable, if quarrelsome, commander, had been killed by artillery fire at Chancellorsville, shortly after Jackson received his wound.

With the return of General Ewell, we got a superb fighter and someone nearly as eccentric as Jackson. He'd lost a leg at Groveton earlier in the war and spent a good deal of the upcoming campaign riding in an open carriage. Well into middle-age, the bald-headed old soldier had just gotten married, which resulted in great comment among the men. In the excitement of battle, he sometimes spoke with a lisp.

On June 4, the Army of Northern Virginia started the march that would lead us into Pennsylvania. The Second Corps broke camp around Fredericksburg and moved west on the Orange Turnpike toward Culpeper.

Here, I began my duties as a courier in earnest. It was a warm and dusty day and Jackson had me dashing in all directions with orders for this regiment to close-up or to find out why General so-and-so had halted his troops without orders. By the evening, my backside ached and I must have met every officer in the corps.

Our army passed through the Chancellorsville battlefield and I rode beside the talkative Jed Hotchkiss as he explained the fighting to General Ewell. Dead horses still lay unburied and the debris of war dotted the landscape. The wildness of the country gave it an unnatural and unpleasant feeling.

I took an immense amount of ribbing over my uniform coat. Lee's army marched hard and fought hard; it contained few bandbox soldiers. Most of the men wore a mixture of coarse gray and brown homespun. Battered slouch hats protected them from the sun and rain while a blanket roll, canteen, cartridge box, and well-used musket completed their apparel. The newness of my jacket with its many brass buttons quickly drew comments.

"Hey, sonny," one veteran called, "What kind of coat is that?"

"It is a V.M.I. uniform," I replied seriously.

This brought but a second's pause and then the rejoinder, "Oh! V.M.I., Very Military Infant!" rang out. A gale of laughter followed and I quickly rode away from them, determined to exchange my coat for one of homespun at the earliest opportunity.

During this march, I participated in one of General Jackson's famous Sunday morning prayer services. Most of the staff and General Ewell were present and the scene was not unlike that captured in the famous print, "Stonewall Jackson's Prayers in Camp."

We stayed near Culpeper for a few days. During this time, General James Ewell Brown Stuart held a grand review of his cavalry, which General Jackson attended with General Lee. This was my first glimpse of the great Southern horseman and he lived up to his reputation. With his plumed hat, fine horse, and gay entourage, he seemed infinitely more colorful than Jackson and, for a time, I wished I could "jine the cavalry." These thoughts passed as the campaign got underway, but Stuart remained my storybook ideal of a soldier.

Major General James Ewell Brown Stuart

A surprise followed the day after the grand review. Yankee cavalry crossed the Rappahannock River and at tacked Stuart's camp near Brandy Station. Their object was to discern and disrupt the movements of our army. In a stiff fight, our men drove the Yankees back across the river.

Maj. Gen. Jubal Anderson Early

Jackson personally led a brigade of infantry to the scene although they were not needed. Here I got my first, distant glimpse of a real battlefield with its thundering cannon, swirling horsemen, and billowing clouds of smoke.

As we observed the action, an ambulance passed carrying General Rooney Lee, who had suffered a serious wound. Rooney was the son of Robert E. Lee. Later on, a Yankee raiding party carried him off from his sickbed at the family home and imprisoned him. The Northern Government felt it quite a coup to capture a convalescent who could not defend himself.

On the afternoon of June 10, the day following the battle at Brandy Station, Jackson's Corps resumed its movement north. In several days of pleasant marching, we passed through the Blue Ridge at Chester's Gap, forded the south branch of the Shenandoah River, and continued past Front Royal toward Winchester. The Yankee general, Milroy, was determined to make his stand at that place.

South of town, we encountered the enemy and sharp fighting ensued. General Jackson sent me galloping off to the left of the Valley Turnpike with instructions for General Early. I took a short cut and found myself caught between some retreating Federals and our skirmishers. I turned to retrace my steps, but several Yankee soldiers blocked my escape.

I drew my pistol, spurred my horse, and rode directly into them. Neither they nor I fired a shot. They were as eager to get past me as I was to get past them. My escapade brought cheers from our lines, and, when word got to headquarters, I suffered a great deal of ribbing. For the remainder of the war, my nickname was "Flash."

As a result of the fighting, a big, black gelding, that belonged to a Yankee officer, came into my hands. This was fortunate, for my little roan needed relief from the constant demands of active courier duty. I nicknamed the gelding "Old Abe" and I took particular delight in the silver-mounted Mexican saddle that was captured with him.

A rainstorm swept in that evening and gave the enemy an opportunity to withdraw into rifle pits north of town. Our troops slept on their weapons along the line of battle.

The dawn was cloudy and overcast, but the sun broke through about mid-day. General Jackson spent most of the morning atop a ridge overlooking the Yankee earthworks, directing the placement of the troops. At one point, he put down his field glasses and said to no one in particular, "This is the Sabbath and I never like to fight on the Sabbath. May Providence crown our arms with victory." Later, he even took a brief nap while waiting for his troop dispositions to be completed.

During this time, a courier arrived and handed the General a message. He glanced at it quickly and mumbled, "Now, the circle is complete." Then he returned to his slumbers.

Though Jackson did not tell us, Stuart's cavalry had arrived east of Winchester, effectively blocking Milroy's escape.

Just about five o'clock, all was in readiness. Our troops had moved, unobserved, to a position west of the Yankee fortifications and began a terrific cannonade. This punishment continued for some time until Hay's Louisiana brigade rushed the westernmost set of earthworks. These quickly fell, with many prisoners taken, though some Yankees escaped into their main fort. Artillery fire continued until darkness ended the contest.

After such an exhausting day, I looked forward to some peaceful hours of rest. This was not be. I had no sooner lay down on my blanket when Jackson had me roused to carry orders to General Ewell. Jackson foresaw the enemy's escape attempt and wanted to tighten the noose.

That night, Milroy tried to move his troops toward Harper's Ferry. He collided with our forces near Stephenson's Depot. Milroy's army was shattered and Milroy himself escaped capture only by fleeing across the fields on a firm-footed stallion.

Jackson had achieved complete victory. Over 4,000 prisoners, twenty-three cannons, and a great quantity of wagons and stores were captured. The General received an ovation as he entered Winchester to set up headquarters in the Taylor Hotel. He had many friends among the populace, thanks to his previous stays in the area, and he spent much of the day receiving visitors.

Among the staff, we debated what our next move would be. Several senior members stated flatly that we would "gobble up" the Federal garrison at Harper's Ferry in a repeat of Jackson's triumph during the Sharpsburg campaign. Others expected us to threaten Washington and Hooker's rear. A third opinion had us marching straight to Pennsylvania. Jackson, of course, stayed silent on the subject.

That afternoon, the plan began to reveal itself. Jackson met with Stuart, Ewell, and several of the other senior officers. Stuart, with two brigades of horsemen, would lead the way into Pennsylvania. The rest of the cavalry corps, under Fitzhugh Lee, remained on the other side of the Blue Ridge to screen the army's movement. The Second Corps would follow Stuart and the First Corps would be last.

Contrary to what certain other histories of the war claim, it was General Jackson who suggested to General Lee that Stuart lead the invasion. Jackson trusted Stuart implicitly and felt comfortable with him in the advance. Moreover, Stuart knew the area from his raid into Pennsylvania the

previous autumn. His presence also led the Northern commanders to believe our movement was nothing more than
the cavalry foray that had been widely predicted by the
Yankee newspapers.[4]

The troops began their march before daybreak on June
16th. The advance traveled as far as Shepherdstown on the
Potomac River. Jackson spent the morning paying calls and
doing paperwork before moving the headquarters to Bunker
Hill for the evening. General Early stayed behind for a day
to parole prisoners and secure supplies.

On the 18th, Jackson transferred his headquarters into
Maryland. We camped at the home of Henry Kyd Douglas,
who had served on Jackson's staff in the early part of the
war. The house was a fine structure, but it had been much
abused by the enemy.

We remained in the area several days. The Chesapeake
and Ohio Canal was destroyed, supplies were gathered, and
some of the troops made feints toward Harper's Ferry. I visited the battlefield around Sharpsburg and accompanied Jed
Hotchkiss on a map-making expedition to Williamsport.
While there, we learned that Stuart had reached Chambersburg, Pennsylvania; we knew that we would soon follow.

---

[4] Stuart leading the advance remains a subject of controversy. Some maintain he should
have been sent behind the Federal Army to cut its communication with Washington.

Built in 1798, Peace Church, near Camp Hill, Pennsylvania, was the position of Confederate artillery during the fight for Pennsylvania's capital. (Cumberland County Historical Society)

Chapter Three

INTO PENNSYLVANIA

We crossed the Mason-Dixon line with slight fanfare on June 22, 1863. General Jackson rode in an ambulance, studying maps. Behind us, a regimental band struck up "Yankee Doodle" as the soldiers straightened their ragged ranks, swung their muskets to right shoulder shift, and made their official entrance "back into the Union."

It was a veritable land of milk and honey after what we had seen in poor, war-torn Virginia. There were prosperous farms with big stone barns and houses, many of which were occupied by Dutch folk who spoke little English.

While we were under strict orders not to loot, a good deal of foraging and requisitioning went on. Stuart's cavalry, ranging far ahead, sent back a steady stream of horses and cattle.

Even General Jackson went shopping. In Greencastle, he put a few lemons into his leather haversack and paid Confederate money to the unhappy merchant, who did not recognize his famous customer.

Also in Greencastle, several sour-looking women with the old, grid-iron colors pinned to their bosoms, exchanged jibes with the passing troops. Their fun ended when I heard one old soldier say, "Look out, ladies! We Rebs are pretty good at taking Yankee flags off breastworks."

Here the men began the amusing game of exchanging headgear with civilian on-lookers. Many a Rebel traded his weather-beaten, old, slouch hat for one of the fine new chapeaus worn by the Yankee gentlemen. My own hat was in good shape but the game looked like such fun that I, too, participated. I snatched three or four coverings off unsuspecting Yankee pates and passed them into the ranks before the General noticed and ordered me to stop.

By now, Jackson had split the corps to conduct one of the most brilliant marches of his career. Early moved east, across the South Mountains, toward York and the Susquehanna River. Jackson, along with the remainder of the corps, moved up the Cumberland Valley, following the trail of Stuart's cavalry. Depending upon the fortunes of war, the corps planned to rendezvous in Harrisburg, Pennsylvania's capital at that time.

We spent three days around Chambersburg, a nice-sized town that served as the seat of Franklin County. A crowd gathered to see the mighty "Stonewall" as we entered the town square and several onlookers expressed disappointment in the warrior's well-worn appearance. A local resident, Jacob Hoke, wrote:

> *We keenly anticipated the arrival of the great Rebel chieftain. Each passing officer was asked when Jackson would appear. Finally, he rode into the diamond and the disappointment was almost universal. Before us was an average man of average height, mounted on an indifferent chestnut horse. Under other circumstances, his dusty uniform would not have been suitable garb to permit his admittance into the Franklin Hotel, which he entered. A rebel flag was run out the window and headquarters established.*

To these remarks, consider the comment of a Yankee prisoner captured at Harper's Ferry a year before. The Yankee said of Jackson, "He ain't much to look at, boys, but, if he was ours, we wouldn't be here."

In the hotel parlor, Dr. Hunter McGuire changed the bandage which still covered Jackson's wounded hand. We then enjoyed an excellent luncheon repast.

Our troops were dispersed strategically about the town and the General kept me occupied running messages all afternoon. I did some shopping, using a Virginia bank note to purchase coffee, even though I did not drink the beverage at that time. Coffee was such a rarity in the Confederacy that I simply felt I should buy some while the opportunity presented itself.

Jackson, once his work was completed, spent the afternoon reading a dime novel which he had found in the hotel parlor. After Jackson put the book down, another officer picked it up and the novel seemed to work its way through the entire army. I last saw it being read by a teamster, near the end of the campaign.

During our stay, a local photographer approached Sandie Pendleton about taking General Jackson's likeness. Sandie felt certain the General would refuse. Earlier that spring, he had posed in camp and then only after he had been led to believe that General Lee would not have his photo taken unless Jackson did likewise.

Sandie enlisted Doctor McGuire's assistance to entrap Jackson for the Chambersburg photographer. The two approached Jackson about coming with them to the "doctor's office" where a picture would be taken to determine if his head injury had healed properly. Jackson was skeptical but gave way before Doctor McGuire's experienced counsel. The resulting photo was perhaps the best likeness of how "Old Jack" really appeared, but a mob of angry Unionists destroyed the plate when our army left town.[5]

The next day, our headquarters moved from the comfort of the Franklin Hotel to the grounds of a Colonel McClure's house north of town. McClure was an officer in the Pennsylvania militia who fled at our advance.

During his stay at the hotel, Jackson had been besieged by curious on-lookers and applicants who either wanted his

[5] The same photographer attempted to take a photo of Lee standing in Chambersburg's square several days later, but the view of his second floor camera was blocked by wagons.

autograph or their horses returned. One woman begged for a lock of the General's hair, confessing that she was a staunch Unionist but would like the souvenir anyway. Jackson demurred.

When headquarters moved to McClure's, the visitor problem lessened but did not completely disappear and General Jackson frequently fled to the safe haven of his tent.

At Hunter McGuire's recommendation, we requisitioned Colonel McClure's stylish carriage for General Jackson's use. Jackson protested but, once again, gave in to Doctor McGuire. Thus, both Generals Jackson and Ewell spent much of the campaign touring the Pennsylvania countryside in civilian comfort. Jackson's carriage also became a great favorite with the staff who frequently invented reasons to deliver lengthy reports sitting beside the General in his vehicle. This continued until a few weeks later, when the carriage broke an axle crossing a rocky stream.

One day I accompanied some of our men on a foraging expedition in the hills to the west. The captain in charge, whose name I no longer recall, had a good set of field glasses, which he used to scout out a place before we went in. He saw one poor farmer dumping hay from a wagon in an attempt to conceal the entrance to the lower level of his bank barn. How this old man cursed when we went directly to the spot where his horses were hidden! His wife cursed even better than he did and she grew more foul when our men began laughing at her rough language. The farm couple seemed not the least bit comforted by the receipt we gave them from Jeff Davis' government.

All in all, history does not record an invading army which behaved better in an enemy's territory. Homes we entered only with permission from their owners. Meals we paid for in our country's currency. Receipts were given for goods requisitioned. Yes, the fruit trees were picked clean, some hats were "exchanged" and a few fellows even got good deals on a watch or two but all this was nothing compared to the destruction that had taken placed in dear old Virginia.

There is one scene, however, which haunts me even today and that was the capture of negroes to be sent back to slavery. Many of these were freed men, living and working in the north, but our army swept up as many as we could. They were then marched south in a pitiful procession. Defenders of the faith may criticize me for writing this, but our army was wrong in making these captures.

From Chambersburg, we moved up the Cumberland Valley through Shippensburg and into the delightful old town of Carlisle, reaching that place on June 27. Here we met General Stuart, whose horsemen were camped at the U. S. Army barracks east of town. General Jackson conferred with Stuart for some time and, later that afternoon, the cavalry moved toward Harrisburg. Stuart was elated to be given the chance to capture the capital of the Keystone State.

The Second Corps had a fine time in Carlisle. Although they were our enemies, the townspeople treated us well and General Jackson attended services at the Presbyterian Church. As was his custom, he slept through much of the sermon, including a prayer for the President of the United States.

In the late afternoon of June 29, General Jackson gave me orders to carry to General Stuart, who was then thought to be on the west bank of the Susquehanna River near Harrisburg. I thrilled at the assignment. Carrying important messages through the enemy countryside was the kind of adventure I'd daydreamed about while working in my father's store back in Lexington. I mounted "Old Abe" and rode off.

The booming of Stuart's artillery directed my path. By dusk, I encountered some of our men gathered around a large stone church[6] which had been turned into a field hospital. They directed me toward the sound of battle where they

---

[6] Peace Church near Shiremanstown.

said I would find Stuart. I rode through the debris of war, over some earthworks, and beheld a magnificent spectacle.

Before me in the twilight lay the Susquehanna River and beyond that the city of Harrisburg with its prominent capitol building. The capitol had been set ablaze and the devilish inferno lit the skyline. I rode across a long, wooden bridge into the city, which was alive with soldiers and panicky civilians. In the town square, I found William Blackford, of Stuart's staff, supervising the parole of some New York militia. Blackford took me to Stuart, who sat on his horse, watching our soldiers fight the fire at the state house. Stuart was in his element, issuing orders right and left and tapping his saddle in time to the banjo and fiddle music that always seemed to surround him.

I handed Jackson's message to Stuart and congratulated him on his victory.

"Yes, I am disappointed that Governor Curtin did not stay to welcome us. Very poor manners for a chief executive, so I have appointed General Wade Hampton military governor of Pennsylvania. You must congratulate him when you see him. He is the first Carolinian to hold the post." Stuart then pointed to the burning building. "This we had no hand in. Their militia did it."[7]

I asked about another large fire visible to the north.

"Oh, that's the Yankee Army's Camp Curtin. Now that we did burn!"

Stuart broke the seal and read the document I had given him. Then he turned to Blackford. "We must work quickly. General Jackson wants us to return to Carlisle. Poor Hampton won't have much time to enjoy his governorship. Let me write a note for General Jackson so he knows of our achievement here."

[7] Exactly how the state house caught fire remains a subject of controversy. Stuart's statement in Randolph's account adds weight to the evidence that the Confederates were not responsible. Like Stuart, some historians blame stragglers from the various northern militias defending the capitol; others believe the blaze began when the Governor's confidential military correspondence was being burned in a first-floor fireplace.

Old Pennsylvania State House
(Courtesy of the Pennsylvania State Archives, Harrisburg, Pennsylvania.)

Stuart swung his leg over the saddle, pulled out his notebook and began writing with a small, gold pencil. I expected him to hand me the dispatch but, instead, he spoke a few words to one of his couriers and the rider galloped away.

"Now Randolph, you rest a spell and you can accompany us back to Carlisle. It's a lovely night for a ride, isn't it?" Then Stuart turned his attention to other matters. I went over into the trees of the capitol park and quickly fell to slumber.

With the first fringe of dawn, I awoke. The cavalry had gone. Except for a few citizens surveying the smoking shell of the state house, I was alone. I mounted my horse and rode through town to the river. Harrisburg had suffered badly in the fighting. Store windows were smashed and their contents strewn through the streets. Gangs of paroled Northern soldiers prowled about and the civil authorities were not visible. I drew my pistol and rode quickly toward the river bridge only to find it ablaze. Across the Susquehanna, Stuart's rear guard could be seen watching the flames.

A gang of Harrisburg plug-uglies gathered along the shore and they eyed me with interest. It took little imagination to foresee the quick revenge they might extract from a lone Confederate soldier. Without hesitation, I spurred my steed into the water.[8]

The river was broad but shallow and I forded it easily. Only in a few spots was it necessary for my horse to swim. Nevertheless, I emerged on the western shore soaked to the skin. What's more, the water ruined the coffee I had purchased a few days earlier.

Harrisburg never recovered from the fighting. The state legislature voted, the following year, to rebuild the capitol in the more central location of Altoona. Its glory gone, Harrisburg declined into the sleepy little river town that it is today.

---

[8] Randolph was fortunate. Two other Confederate stragglers were hung in Market Square and another was shot after they had been captured by the enraged residents.

With Stuart's rear guard, I retraced my route toward Carlisle. Near the town of Mechanicsburg, shots were fired at us and we returned the compliment at the fleeing bushwhackers. At least, the others returned fire. Fording the river, my pistol became wet and now it refused to shoot. Had it not belonged to my father, my rage was such that I would have tossed the worthless iron into the bushes.

In Mechanicsburg, we enjoyed a luncheon of homemade bread and fresh strawberry jam. We found several Philadelphia newspapers with their accounts of "Stuart's Raid" into Pennsylvania and predictions that General Couch would soon overtake the rebels. The opposite was true. General Couch now rode as our prisoner, having been captured when the New York militia fled from their earthworks.

We also encountered an ambulance containing Heros Von Borcke, a German who served on Stuart's staff. Von Borcke had been badly injured in the fighting around Harrisburg and the severity of his wounds finally necessitated that he be left behind. He fell into the enemy's hands, was exchanged, and, though he never recovered sufficiently to return to the field, his reputation grew as one of Richmond's social lions during the winter of 1864.

We reached Carlisle in early afternoon, but Jackson's Corps had already left the town. The citizens greeted us warmly as some stragglers had been making life miserable since Jackson's departure. Stuart quickly restored order and then we followed Jackson's route, marching south toward Gettysburg.

Lt. General Thomas J. Jackson and staff

Chapter Four

THE BATTLE OF GETTYSBURG

Leaving Carlisle, I rode alongside General Stuart, who was still in fine fettle. Though he could not have had more than a few hours' sleep, Stuart maintained a running monologue about the beauties of the Pennsylvania countryside, occasionally requesting a tune from his musicians.

In Papertown, Stuart paused to tour the factory and, as Jackson had done before him, requisitioned several thousand dollars' worth of military forms. We passed through the town of Petersburg and turned onto the Gettysburg Pike, continuing our march until the wee hours of July 1. Outside the village of Heildersburg, we met Rodes' division and camped with them.

After a brief nap, Stuart roused me and we went together to General Jackson's headquarters. We found the General washing his face at a pump in front of a farmhouse. He greeted us cordially and the two commanders engaged in an animated discussion of the military situation. Indeed, it was a curious affair to see General Jackson inform General Stuart on the whereabouts of the armies for it was usually the cavalry general who provided the information.

An argument can be made that General Jackson should not have allowed Stuart to continue on to Carlisle and Harrisburg but should have sent him east through Cashtown Gap to follow the progress of Hooker's Army. However, had he done so, it is unlikely our army would have achieved the strategic coup of capturing Pennsylvania's capital.

The two commanders sat, Indian-style, on the ground and Jackson drew a map in the dirt.

"Generals Lee and Longstreet are coming through the mountains from Chambersburg. Some of Longstreet's men may well be in Cashtown or Gettysburg now. General Early has returned from York and our Second Corps is concentrated right here."

"Did Early cross the Susquehanna?"

"No, the Yankees burned the bridge at Wrightsville."

"Well, we burned the bridge at Harrisburg," Stuart replied jovially. "What of Hooker's army?"

"Hooker has been replaced by General Meade. We believe they are still in Maryland but may cross the line anytime. There have been cavalry skirmishes."

"With Fitz Lee? Where is the rest of my cavalry?"

Jackson shook his head, "I do not know. I don't think they are up yet."

This disturbed Stuart. Fitz Lee's cavalry had been roughly handled in fighting around Upperville, Virginia, while trying to screen the army's northward movement. Only the intervention of our infantry had stopped the Yankees from breaking through the gaps in the Blue Ridge. Now Fitz Lee's command tried to work its way north, tagging along behind on roads clogged by Longstreet's men.

"I hate to fight with one boot off," Stuart said.

"Today, take your men toward Gettysburg and see if the enemy is there. I expect to hear from General Lee at anytime and will let you know what to do."

"I can move within an hour, but my men have had little sleep in the past several days."

"Let them rest a spell, but then move quickly. Your scouts...."

"They are already out."

"Good. Now, General, let me look at you with your new laurels as the hero of Harrisburg. I imagine the Richmond newspapers are already printing your praises."

"Nothing like how they shall praise you after we whip the Yankees this time."

The interview being over, Stuart galloped off. I found a quiet spot in an orchard to nap until Jackson began the day's march.

We had been underway but a short time when a message came from General Longstreet, bringing word that he was at Cashtown with his advance brigades nearing Gettysburg. Jackson sent me off to General Rodes with orders for him to head for the latter point.

I found Rodes close to Gettysburg, where the sound of battle could already be heard. Rodes had learned of Longstreet's arrival and was marching to his support. A courier was en route to Jackson with this news so Rodes asked that I remain with him and carry back any later messages.

We reached the crest of a hill near town and could see off toward the west where the Federals had engaged Longstreet. Rodes studied the scene through his field glasses and then ordered up artillery to enfilade the enemy line. This caught the Yankees by surprise and Rodes turned to one of his officers and said, "We shall make this another Manassas."

But, from the town, Union reinforcements arrived and the Federals fighting Longstreet shifted their lines to accommodate us. Indeed, they appeared about to advance. General Rodes, his blue eyes blazing, ordered an attack, but it was a failure from beginning to end. There was no coordination between the units. O'Neal's Brigade attacked first, losing nearly half their men. General Iverson's brigade followed but the brave North Carolinians also marched into a perfect slaughter from which only four hundred of the 1400 returned.

Later, while I was riding with General Rodes, he noticed what appeared to be an entire regiment lying down in line of battle to escape enemy gunfire. He was about to order them to their feet when he realized they were all dead, casualties of this attack.

Confederate soldier

Daniel and Ramseur brought their soldiers in next. Ramseur, prominent on his large gray horse, appeared to follow the same deadly route as Iverson, and General Rodes sent me forward with orders to shift his line. Before I reached him, however, some of Iverson's men warned Ramseur to correct course. This did give me the opportunity to fire my pistol several times, the first shots I ever fired during battle.

The situation looked grim and General Rodes was much distressed. The Yankees seemed intent on holding their line. Then we heard a cheer and a whoop and looked to see a new attack by Longstreet's men. Soon thereafter, Ewell and Early came with their troops on our left. The Federal line wobbled and broke as our army rushed toward Gettysburg. Surveyed from the ridge, it was a panorama of Southern victory.

We gathered up a great many prisoners from the Army of the Potomac's woeful Eleventh Corps. These were the same people General Jackson had humiliated just two months earlier at Chancellorsville.

Hordes of blue and butternut soldiers fought through the main thoroughfares of Gettysburg. Ahead of us, the streets were blocked with fleeing bluecoats. Yankee artillery tried to slow our advance but, inevitably, they had no choice except to withdraw or be destroyed.

Union Dead left on the field at Gettysburg

The sights of the field were most hideous. Dead men lay crumpled in every manner. Some suffered through their final agonies, screaming and cursing. Others passed their last moments in brave silence. Wounded men worked their way to makeshift field hospitals while injured horses, broken cannons, and all the accouterments of war dotted the fields. Fences and crops lay flat, swept asunder in the whirlwind of violence.

I emptied my canteen several times to help the wounded during that hot July day. Then I saw General Jackson coming down the pike, and I rode to join him.

"A great victory, General!" I chirped.

"Yes, but we must press them," he replied grimly, spurring his horse onward.

Major General Richard S. Ewell

It was now late afternoon and our troops were much pleased with our success. We rode into the town square where a group of officers gathered, General Ewell and General Early being among them. One of the younger officers quickly hid a bottle of wine at Jackson's approach.

General Early waved a hand of welcome. "A most glorious day, General Jackson. Look, toward the mountains. The sun of Gettysburg, sir, the sun of Gettysburg."[9]

Jackson asked, "How far have we chased them?"

"They are on the heights below town," Ewell said.

"Then we have much to do before the sun sets. We must press them, sir. We must press them."

"Our men are disorganized by the chase through town," Early replied.

"No more so than the enemy we have defeated."

At this point, Stuart appeared and reported that his command rested on the army's left and could advance when ordered. Stuart also asked permission to go after the enemy's cavalry, which was in that area.

"See!" Jackson exclaimed, "General Stuart is ready to fight. General Ewell, organize your men and prepare for an assault on the enemy position. Come on, let us scout their lines ourselves."

---

[9] Early's words echo those of Napoleon at Austerlitz.

We traveled south from the square. Gunfire continued to our front and I began to doubt the wisdom of going much further. But Jackson was unconcerned and rode on, sucking his lemon.

Before us, we saw a gradual knoll, known locally as Cemetery Hill. Here the Yankees were milling about, throwing up breastworks and placing cannons. Jackson surveyed their line silently. Then we zigzagged through the back streets of town to get a look from another angle. Ewell and Early still accompanied us and we were shortly joined by Rodes, who brought word that General Lee and General Longstreet were en route.

Our cavalcade soon attracted the attention of Yankee artillery and we moved back into the town, taking shelter behind the county prison. A courier arrived and said that General Johnson's division could reach the field, if needed, for service that evening.

Jackson told the courier to have Johnson come at the double quick; however, Jackson did not propose to wait for reinforcements before assaulting the heights. Scouts told us that Birney's Division of the Army of the Potomac's Third Corps had arrived and more bluecoats could be seen marching north on the Emmitsburg Pike. With each passing hour, the enemy grew stronger.

Jackson led the group into the shade of the trees where he dismounted and entered quiet discussion with Ewell, Rodes and Early. After a few minutes, the conference dispersed. Chaplain Lacy appeared with a jug of chilled buttermilk, which we all enjoyed. Out the York Road, sounds of battle told us Stuart had found the enemy cavalry.

As the minutes slowly passed, Jackson grew apprehensive and consulted his watch frequently. Several times he sent messages off to hurry the assault. In the meantime, the staff organized an impromptu picnic of bread and cheese. The Pennsylvania Dutch made very good bread.

Lee and Jackson met together to plan their strategy
for the coming day.

Around seven o'clock, General Lee joined us. He and Jackson walked off by themselves and then returned with orders for us to mount. We rode southeast of town to General Early's lines where we could get a good glimpse of Cemetery Heights. It looked, to me, like a fearsome position and, had I not felt fully confident of our army, I would have believed we had little hope of success.

General Early rode up and saluted General Lee and General Jackson.

"Now you're going to see some fighting!" Early exclaimed after Jackson nodded to his request to advance.

It was a scene that I shall never forget, one that has yet to be adequately depicted in any painting. Early's men marched with shouldered rifles into the glowing red twilight. The sun's dying rays glinted off their bayonets and their battle flags shook with anticipation. A Rebel yell rose and fell, and it almost seemed enough to make the bluecoat line tremble. To our right, Ewell and Rodes could be seen moving en echelon. Ahead, the Yankee cannons began to boom.

I looked to General Lee. He sat erect, astride Traveller, with field glasses in his hands. His handsome face showed all the strength and confidence of his character; there was something like a father's fierce pride evident as he watched his men move in.

Jackson, too, watched silently, slumped in the saddle and still cradling his watch in his hand. Both men were quiet except for one instance when General Jackson pointed and said, simply, "Louisiana." Lee nodded; then they continued their vigil in silence. At one point, a cannonball splintered a tree directly behind us, but this stray shot passed unnoticed and un-remarked upon by the two commanders. All that mattered lay to the front.

Union artillery

Early's men made it halfway up the hill, Ewell's went a little farther, and Rodes' assault seemed to falter from the start. Lee and Jackson stiffened as our men fell back under the punishing artillery and gunfire.

Without consulting Lee, Jackson turned to me and said, "Tell General Early to go again." I turned to leave and saw General Johnson approaching. General Lee shook Johnson's hand, which reminded me of my error the first time I met

Lee. Jackson quickly sketched the situation and I went to Early with the glad tidings that his next assault would be supported by a fresh division.

The troops had retired in good order and I rode among them until I found General Early sitting on a rock and engaged in an animated conversation with General Gordon.

Early spied me and waved a welcoming hand, "Come on, boy. Let me guess the news from Old Jack."

Breathless from my rapid ride, I blurted, "General Jackson wishes you to renew your assault on the enemy."

Early spat a stream of tobacco juice. "See! I told you, Gordon. My men have had a day full of victory, but we cannot possibly take that hill without reinforcement."

Gordon began to speak but I interrupted him. "General Johnson has arrived and will support you in your attack."

At this Early brightened and exclaimed, "If Johnson is up and ready, you tell Jackson that we'll drink our whiskey in that cemetery tonight. General Gordon, are you ready?"

General Gordon jumped like a gamecock at the question. "General, tonight we'll be in the cemetery one way or the other." Then Gordon grinned at me and asked, "Do you want to go along? It may be the last charge of the war."

"Yes, sir."

Early spat again and shook his head. "No. He goes back to Jackson. Now come on, Gordon. You wanted to go back up there. Here's your chance. And, you, you go back and give Jackson my message. If Johnson comes up, we'll gain the hill."

"Well, look yonder, General. There are Johnson's men now," Gordon said.

Barely visible in failing light, the fresh division wheeled into line.

Reader, have you ever traveled easily in daylight and then attempted to retrace your steps in the darkness? Familiar countryside can become confusing territory as you attempt to distinguish any friendly landmark. This is what happened to me now. For nearly an hour, I blundered about, looking for General Jackson. I found him just after the second attack began.

In the darkness, the assault was all fireworks and confusion. From our vantage, it was difficult to gauge our success or failure, but the shadows seemed to draw near and merge in a calliope of shots, screams, and cheers.

Then, in an instant, the result became clear. We had taken the hill and the enemy was in flight.

"Come on," Jackson barked. We ran quickly to the heights, attempting to avoid the dead and wounded who dotted the field. The fighting was still progressing and several officers urged Jackson to fall back but he would have none of it. I took the opportunity to empty my revolver into the retreating Yankees. In a few minutes, the remnants of the Union resistance ended.

Near the crest of the slope, General Jackson dismounted to minister to a wounded soldier and, riding closer, I recognized Henry Kyd Douglas, whose family home we had visited after crossing the Potomac. Douglas had been on Jackson's staff, but went on to command a company of the famous Stonewall Brigade. He then joined General Johnson as assistant adjutant general. Now he lay in his old commander's arms, suffering from a serious shoulder wound.

I excused myself and went towards the cemetery gate house where I found Generals Lee and Longstreet. They asked of General Jackson's whereabouts and I quickly fetched him. What followed was the moonlight conference so famous in Gettysburg folklore.[10]

The three generals rode some distance to the Taneytown Road, stopping at a small, white, frame, farm house. Here they found the casualties and debris of battle not so apparent. A chair was brought for General Lee and a small fire

[10] The farm house was owned by a widow named Leister and it stood in the vicinity of the present-day shopping center. Little of the battlefield has been preserved although the cemetery gate house still stands.

built. Jackson reclined on the porch while Longstreet stood and frequently paced about with his arms folded behind him. Most of the staff remained at a respectful distance but it was not difficult to understand their discussion.

Lee first asked about the pursuit of the beaten Federals and Jackson replied that Early and Ewell were in the advance. Longstreet indicated that a fresh division under General McLaws was moving across the fields toward the Emmitsburg Pike.

"Where is our cavalry?" Lee asked. "Where is Stuart?"

Jackson began to speak, but was interrupted by the appearance of a courier who handed General Lee a note from the commander in question. I reproduce it here as it appears in the Official Records:

> *July 1*
> *9:30 p.m.*
>
> *General:*
> *We encountered the enemy's cavalry this evening south of the York Road.*
> *Following a fierce battle, we have gained a decided advantage and will pursue it to the fullest extent. My troops are bloodied but full of fight.*
>
> *Yr. ob. srvt.,*
> *J.E.B. Stuart*
> *Major General*

As stated earlier, General Stuart was a commander whom I greatly admired and respected. Nevertheless, he had his faults and this note displays one of them. It is true that Stuart had encountered the enemy south of the York Road. It is true that a fierce battle had been fought in the twilight. But it is not true that our cavalry gained a "decided advantage." Indeed, at 9:30 p.m., both sets of horsemen rested in place, like two tuckered hound dogs after a scrap. The record shows that General Kilpatrick did not withdraw his troops until nearly midnight, after receiving word from General Hancock of the Union disaster on Cemetery Hill. Otherwise, Kilpatrick probably would have remained in place to fight Stuart again come the sunrise.

General Lee carefully folded the note and handed it to Major Marshall.[11] "Well, Stuart is busy with the enemy's cavalry, so we have no horsemen to follow up our victory." He then looked wistfully to the south where our infantry continued to engage the fleeing men of Hancock and Howard. One can only imagine the consternation a mounted division could have created.

Lee accepted a map from Marshall and lay it on the ground near the fire, anchoring one end with a piece of grapeshot and the other with a discarded shoe. Jackson and Longstreet drew nearer and their conversation was softer, though I believe Lee quizzed them on the events of the day. General Pendleton, Sandie Pendleton's father, joined the group as did General Trimble, who was without command. These officers said little throughout the remainder of the conference.

After a few minutes, Lee pointed to the map and declared, "It was always my belief that the battle would come either near this town or at Frederick. Now that those people have been beaten here, they cannot leave Baltimore uncovered. General Meade has a rail line to Westminster so he will most likely look for a defensive position along here in northern Maryland."

Longstreet put his finger at another point on the map, "Let's move west and make Meade attack us in the mountain passes."

Lee shook his head, "No. We cannot allow General Meade to fight us in his own good time. He is new to command and we have seriously damaged his army. We must follow our advantage."

---

[11] Randolph is probably not correct here. Most other sources indicate Lee put the note in his left vest pocket.

Jackson grunted in agreement.

General Pendleton asked a question about the train and Longstreet said something about wagons being "strung out from here to Chambersburg."

Lee replied, "If the situation is as I believe it to be, our trains should concentrate near Emmitsburg, for our army will be beyond that point tomorrow. General Jackson, regroup your command and move toward Taneytown and Westminster. General Longstreet, you will march to Emmitsburg and turn to the southeast. We'll feel out the enemy's position. Stuart shall remain on the army's left."

Longstreet said, "It might take some time. Some of my troops are still on the Chambersburg Pike."

"Move with what you have and tell the others to hurry along."

General Jackson looked as if he were asleep but asked, "When do you want me to march?"

"How soon can you?"

"Daybreak."

"Fine. Give your men a good rest tonight but get underway in the early hours."

I listened to the distant gunfire and wondered how our men could get a good rest when some of them were still fighting.

At this, the conference broke up. Jackson sent orders to his division commanders. Fortunately, I was not selected to carry any. General Jackson led the way to a nearby ridge where we camped beneath a grove of trees. I fell asleep instantly, the last shots of the battle of Gettysburg still echoing to the south.

Chapter Five

JULY 2

At this juncture, it may be appropriate to review, for the reader, the overall strategic position of the opposing forces on the morning of July 2.

Since the beginning of the campaign, the Army of Northern Virginia had stolen a march on the Army of the Potomac and our butternut legions had roamed virtually at will throughout southern Pennsylvania.

"Fighting Joe" Hooker gradually realized that the invasion was more than another of Stuart's raids and brought his troops north across the Potomac. Hooker never seriously impeded our movement, although the infantry had to march to Fitz Lee's rescue during a cavalry fight in the mountain gaps near Upperville, Virginia. Had Hooker followed his advantage and crossed the mountains, he would have broken up General Lee's entire plan.

However, on June 28, Hooker lost his command to George Gordon Meade, a capable and hard-fighting general, though nothing on the order of Lee or Jackson.

Gen. George G. Meade

The Federal Army was then in Maryland, and Meade had little time to draw up plans for his campaign. Nevertheless, in remarkably short order, he developed what is known as the Pipe Creek Circular, which I reprint here:

Headquarters
Army of the Potomac
Taneytown, Maryland
July 1, 1863

From the information received, the commanding general is satisfied that the object of the movement of the army in this direction has been accomplished, viz., the enemy has abandoned Harrisburg and been prevented from advancing on Philadelphia. It is no longer his intention to assume the offensive until the enemy's movements or position should render such an operation certain of success.

If the enemy assumes the offensive, and attacks, it is the commanding general's intention, after holding them in check sufficiently long, to withdraw the trains and other impedimenta; to withdraw the army from its present position, and form line of battle with the left resting in the neighborhood of Middleburg, and the right at Manchester, the general direction being that of Pipe Creek. For this purpose, General Reynolds, in command of the left, will withdraw the force present at Gettysburg, two corps by the road to Taneytown and Westminster, and, after crossing Pipe Creek, deploy toward Middleburg. The corps at Emmitsburg will be withdrawn, via Mechanicsville, to Middleburg, or, if a more direct route can be found leaving Taneytown to their left, to withdraw direct to Middleburg.

General Slocum will assume command of the two corps at Hanover and Two Taverns, and withdraw them, via Union Mills, deploying one to the right and one to the left, after crossing Pipe Creek, connecting on the left with General Reynolds, and communicating his right to General Sedgwick at Manchester who will connect with him and form the right.

The time for falling back can only be developed by circumstances. Whenever such circumstances arise as would seem to indicate the necessity for falling back and assuming this general line indicated, notice of such movement will be at once communicated to these headquarters and all adjoining corps commanders.

The Second Corps now at Taneytown will be held in reserve in the vicinity of Uniontown and Frizellburg, to be thrown to the point of strongest attack, should the enemy make it. In the event of these movements being necessary, the trains and impedimenta will be sent to the rear of Westminster.

Corps commanders, with their officers commanding artillery and the divisions, should make themselves thoroughly familiar with the country indicated, all the roads and positions, so that no possible confusion can ensue and that the movement, if made, be done with good order, precision, and care, without loss or any detriment to the morale of the troops.

The commanders of corps are requested to communicate at once the nature of their present positions, and their ability to hold them in the case of any sudden attack at any point by the enemy.

This order is communicated, that a general plan, perfectly understood by all, may be had for receiving attack, if made in strong force, upon any portion of our present position.

Developments may cause the commanding general to assume the offensive from his present positions.

The Artillery Reserve will, in the event of the general movement indicated, move to the rear of Frizellburg, and be placed in position, or sent to corps, as circumstances may require, under the general supervision of the chief of artillery.

The chief quartermaster will, in case of the general movement indicated, give directions for the orderly and proper position of the trains in the rear of Westminster.

All the trains will keep well to the right of the road in moving, and, in case of any accident requiring a halt, the teams must be hauled out of line, and not delay the movements.

The trains ordered to Union Bridge in these events will be sent to Westminster.

General headquarters will be, in case of this movement, at Frizellburg; General Slocum as near Union Mills as the line will render best for him; General Reynolds at or near the road from Taney-town to Frizellburg.

The chief of artillery will examine the line, and select positions for the artillery.

The cavalry will be held on the right and left flanks after the movement is completed. Previous to its completion, it will, as now directed, cover the front and exterior lines, well out.

The commands must be prepared for a movement, and, in the event of the enemy attacking us on the ground indicated herein, to follow up any repulse.

The chief signal officer will examine the line thoroughly, and at once, upon the commencement of this movement, extend telegraphic communication from each of the following points to general headquarters near Frizellburg, viz., Manchester, Union Mills, Middleburg, and Taneytown road.

All true Union people should be advised to harass and annoy the enemy in every way, to send in information, and taught how to do it; giving regiment by number of colors, number of guns, generals' names, &c. All their supplies brought to us will be paid for, and not fall into the enemy's hands.

*Roads and ways to move to the right or the left of
the general line should be studied and thoroughly
understood. All movements of troops should be concealed, and our dispositions kept from the enemy.
Their knowledge of these dispositions would be fatal
to our success, and the greatest care must be taken
to prevent such an occurrence.*
  By command of General Meade:
  S. Williams
  Assistant Adjutant-General

Of course, much had changed in the few hours since this order was drafted.

General Reynolds had been killed in the early hours of the July 1 fighting. The First Corps and the Eleventh Corps had been routed and driven through the streets of Gettysburg. Reinforced by the Twelfth Corps and Birney's Division of the Third Corps, they attempted to make a stand on Cemetery Ridge but, after sharp fighting, were again routed. Indeed, so much of the First and Eleventh Corps had been rendered hors de combat that neither would be an effective fighting force for the remainder of the campaign.

Through the early hours of July 2, General Meade listened with sinking heart as Generals Hancock and Howard recounted the day's disasters. For Howard, it was the final act of his active military service for he resigned after popular opinion blamed him for the defeats at both Chancellorsville and Gettysburg.

General Meade then began gathering what was left of his army to follow the Pipe Creek plan.

It is also worth a moment to examine the state of the Army of Northern Virginia. We were nearly as disorganized by victory as the Army of the Potomac was by defeat. In just a few short weeks, the army had marched from its base deep in Virginia right to the heart of the enemy's country. We had fought major battles at Winchester, Harrisburg, and Gettysburg and now needed to consolidate our triumphs with one last, decisive engagement.

On the morning of July 2, units of our army's First and Second Corps were intermingled along a line that ran raggedly between the Emmitsburg and Baltimore Pikes. The right of the line touched Marsh Creek, nearly at the Maryland border, while the left of the line was north of Littlestown, where our cavalry halted after a comic moonlight skirmish with Kilpatrick's retreating cavalry.

Our line of defense -- if it could be called that -- was by no means sound. Had General Meade attacked with any organized force, he could have rolled us up like a wet blanket. Regiments simply stopped when they'd had enough fighting or too few men to continue.

Adding to the disarray, we held thousands of prisoners -- far more than we were equipped to handle in the enemy's territory. At that moment, they were corralled near the train station in Gettysburg, but their large numbers made them a worrisome threat.

Yet, what were we to do? Parole them and have the enemy not honor the parole because we could not evacuate them from the field? March them through the Cashtown Pass on the long trek back to Virginia, which not only offered ample opportunity for escape but would require guards in such numbers as to seriously detract from our fighting power? What's more, the Cashtown Pass remained blocked with elements of the First Corps and our supply trains.

General Lee decided to parole many of the Union enlisted men with the stipulation that they leave the battlefront immediately. Tables were set up in the town square and at the Lutheran Seminary and, through the day of July 2, the necessary paperwork was issued. Yankee officers went under guard to Virginia.

General Jackson's servant, Jim, awoke me with a cup of coffee at four in the morning and said that the General needed me immediately. Though I disliked coffee, I drank it anyway and went to see the General. He kept me busy for several hours, running dispatches to all parts of the line. One of these was to General Rodes, instructing him to proceed to Taneytown. His troops broke camp some time after eight o'clock and were in Maryland shortly thereafter. General Ewell took the Baltimore Pike toward Littlestown and Westminster at about mid-morning. General Johnson followed Ewell while Early followed Rodes.

General Jackson left Gettysburg at ten o'clock and headed to Taneytown. En route, we passed a farmhouse where a toothless old woman offered us some chicken. Since it was approaching the appropriate hour, the General accepted and we dismounted to have a regular luncheon on her porch.

Some of the boys inquired of her sympathies and she assured us she was as good a Union woman as ever lived but she had a tremendous desire to see the great Stonewall Jackson up close. Then she began hinting that she would like one of the brass buttons off the General's coat as a souvenir.

General Jackson tried to avoid the issue by saying he wished he "had enough buttons to give one to every pretty woman who asked." At the words "pretty woman," a couple members of the staff turned away to hide their amusement.

But the old lady persisted, "Isn't that just about the best chicken you ever tasted, General?"

He assured her it was.

"It's hard for an old woman like me to get along with the war and all. I have just a few chickens but I wanted to have one cooked in case the famous General Jackson came by."

At this, Jackson gave in and cut one of the buttons from his coat. Immediately thereafter, General Lee and his staff appeared. General Lee wore his linen duster over his uniform coat which, despite the heat, he buttoned to the throat. The old lady eyed Lee's double row of gilt buttons and asked if he'd like some chicken. The General accepted and the entire scenario played out again. General Jackson was much amused. This stands as the only recorded incident where both Lee and Jackson were out-maneuvered on the same day.

After lunch, I walked around back where several fruit pies sat cooling just inside the window. Feeling certain our host would not mind, especially if I offered her a button, I greedily and quickly ate an entire pie. Before long, my stomach began to ache and I went to the outhouse. It was occupied so I waited, feeling sicker and sicker. Finally, I banged on the door, "Hurry up in there! There are others in line."

Suddenly the door swung open and General Lee came out. He said nothing to me but walked slowly back around the house. Lee himself seemed ill and I wondered if he, too, had eaten one of the woman's pies.

After our luncheon, the Generals rode together into Taneytown. Beyond the settlement, Rodes' troops could be heard in sporadic skirmishes with the enemy. Gunfire to the west told us that Longstreet's Corps was on the scene as well.

Passing through the town, General Lee halted at a large red brick house and said he expected to establish his headquarters nearby. He instructed Jackson to see to the placement of his troops and determine the enemy's position. They agreed to meet later that afternoon and General Jackson sent me scurrying off to find Longstreet and inform him of our arrival and the proposed conference.

This was not the easiest task. Our troops had clogged the roads in every direction. Not only did I not know where Longstreet was, I wasn't sure where I was. Fortunately, Jed Hotchkiss happened by and let me quickly copy a rough map of the area. Then I rode off toward Emmitsburg.

Along the way, I inquired of each officer I met if he knew where General Longstreet was. One bright fellow told me he was "over the creek, up the ridge and past the big barn on the left side." After I scrawled these imprecise instructions on the back of my map, he offered me a drink from his canteen.

The day was hot, my throat was dry, and my own canteen was empty, so I accepted. I took a long swallow, then realized it was whiskey. I coughed, tried not to gag, and hoped to hide my discomfort from my amused benefactor.

His directions took me right through the fields where our line of battle was forming. I found Longstreet in an exposed position, watching some Yankee batteries on the adjacent ridge. I saluted and handed him the note from General Jackson.

"Well, the Yankees are moving east about as quick as they can," Longstreet said. "Let's go see General Lee." Then Longstreet gave a few orders to his staff on troop placement and we retraced my route to Taneytown. Along the way, Longstreet stopped frequently to scan the distant hills where the bluecoats milled about like so many ants.

I had only seen Longstreet a few times before and had never had the chance to observe him closely. Since the war, I have come to know him quite well and greatly admire his fine character and many abilities.[12]

In the Army of Northern Virginia, Robert E. Lee was revered like no other man. Perhaps the prevailing attitude is best described in the story of two soldiers who argued over Darwin's theory of evolution. Finally, one of the old Confederates threw down his hat in disgust and said, "Well, maybe the rest of us was made from monkeys but there's no way that General Lee was."

Jackson, on the other hand, was viewed as a magnificent eccentric who brought us brilliant victories. His oddities only served to confirm his genius and set him apart from the other men.

---

[12] Randolph had a brief post-war association with Longstreet in the insurance business.

But General Longstreet was a soldier's soldier, someone whom the ordinary fighting man could follow and identify with. While he maintained the dignity and distance required by rank, one could readily imagine Longstreet indulging in a game of cards and a couple of nips, two habits he enjoyed more frequently early in the war before a fatal illness took two of his daughters. One cannot ever imagine General Lee and General Jackson settling in for an enjoyable evening of whiskey and poker.

General Longstreet has been criticized for many things since the war but I know that no officer held the respect of his men and of General Lee any more than "Old Pete."

We passed through Taneytown, still a madhouse of marching troops, and came to the cluster of Lee's headquarters tents. Longstreet joined Lee at a small camp table while I sat wondering where Jackson was. In short order, Lee and Longstreet rose and walked a short distance to see the enemy position. They returned with General Jackson and all three entered Lee's tent for a conference.

This left me with nothing to do, so I let my horse graze in the yard while I curled up in a fence corner for a late afternoon nap.

Just around the time I drifted off, there came a sound that stood out from the other commotion of the marching troops. It was Jeb Stuart with his entourage, all of them singing along as his banjo player plunked out "The Bonnie Blue Flag." General Stuart always had a weakness for a colorful arrival at headquarters.

Stuart dismounted and, spying me in the fence corner, tossed a couple pieces of hard candy in my direction.

"Take this," he said, "It's from General Kilpatrick's headquarters' wagon."

Then Stuart entered the tent to join the conference.

From a reliable source, I have assembled a complete account of that historic meeting.[13] Lee opened the discussion by asking Longstreet, then Jackson, what the dispositions of their troops were vis a vis the enemy. Longstreet had just begun when General Stuart arrived and repeated his performance with the candy.

Maj. Gen. George E. Pickett

Longstreet began again, "My corps is either present or arriving on the field. Pickett's division is still in Pennsylvania but should be up this evening. My line parallels that of the enemy who is moving east on the hills behind the creek. In fact, my corps extends beyond the enemy left."

"Where does your line meet Jackson's?" Lee asked.

"Out yonder on the pike," Longstreet replied and then pointed to the map.

"Who is in your front?"

"Best I can tell, Sickles holds the left. Hancock in the center. Probably somebody else in there, too."

"Do you know, General Stuart?"

"Kilpatrick's cavalry is on the enemy's right. Sedgwick has come up from Manchester."

"Facing Jackson?"

"Facing my cavalry."

"Well, General Jackson, can you help General Stuart?"

"General Johnson is on our left and can hold the Sixth Corps if they come at us. The enemy's Fifth Corps is also there."

---

[13] Probably Longstreet.

"You've scouted their position, General Stuart?"

"Some of it. Good rolling countryside and they're digging in on the ridges. It's a fine defensive position but I reckon we can whip 'em."

"My men are ready to attack tonight," Jackson said.

"Maybe we should wait and let Meade attack us," Longstreet suggested.

"No, General," Lee shook his head, "The enemy is there and I am going to strike him. I want our army to attack in force early tomorrow."

At this, Lee excused himself and left the tent for several minutes.

"You think you can storm their position?" Longstreet asked.

"Their army won't stand a strong attack from ours."

"But, if we wait on the defensive, we could have another Fredericksburg."

"No, General Meade will not do that. Any delay gives him more time to recover from yesterday's defeat. We should attack immediately."

Longstreet thought a moment and then used his finger to draw an arc on the map. "What if I came around here and attacked the enemy's left flank?"

"Can you do it?"

"With a proper guide. I could attack tomorrow morning at the same time you assault their right. We'd roll them right up."

"While I whip their cavalry and cut their retreat," Stuart added.

The discussion continued until General Lee returned and Longstreet presented his flanking proposal.

Lee shook his head, "No, General. There is no time. We must strike the enemy early tomorrow. They cannot hold against our army."

Jackson then seemed to dismiss the flanking movement, "What time can you attack in the morning, General Longstreet?"

"Six. Seven at the latest," Longstreet replied gruffly, surprised that Jackson had not supported his argument for the flanking movement.

Lee turned to Jackson. "When you hear General Longstreet's advance, attack with your whole corps beginning on our left. We'll strike both flanks and then crumple their center. General Stuart, you will swing to the east and get behind them."

The meeting then adjourned. I saw Longstreet leave the tent. He seemed preoccupied and spoke to no one, mounting his horse quickly and riding away.

General Jackson kept me busy the remainder of the evening, running messages hither and yon. There was an electric tension in the air. Our army, poised and confident, girded itself for a stiff fight and sure victory on the morrow. The enemy waited, edgy and nervous, afraid that Bobby Lee would do a double somersault and end up between them and Washington.

Both sides exchanged gunfire throughout the night. At one point, their artillery opened on us as Early's Division came into line. Our artillery responded and a regular cannonade ensued until General Jackson ordered our gunners to stop wasting ammunition.

"The real battle," he said, "will commence tomorrow."

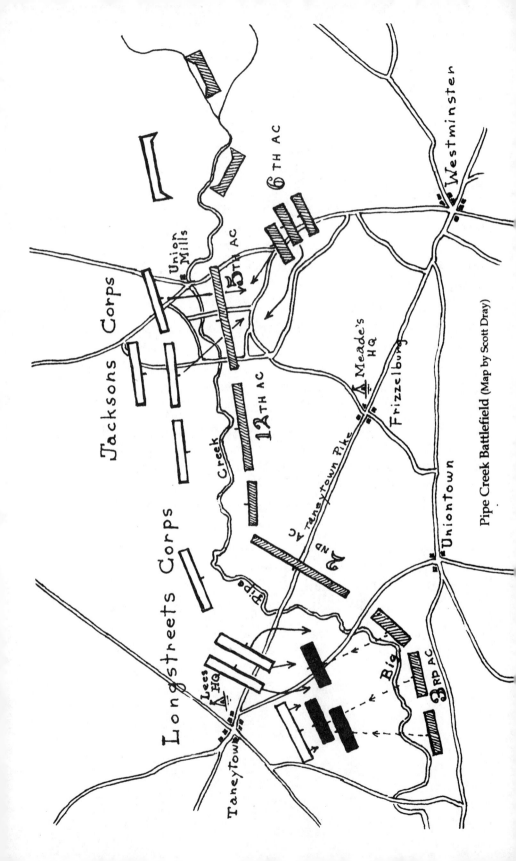

Pipe Creek Battlefield (Map by Scott Dray)

Jacksons Corps

Longstreets Corps

Union Mills

Creek

Pipe

Lee's HQ

Taneytown

Westminster

6 TH AC

5TH AC

12TH AC

Meade's HQ

Frizzelburg

Taneytown Pike

2ND AC

Uniontown

Big

3RD AC

Chapter Six

JULY 3

The sound of cannon fire awoke me on July 3. I was refreshed and ready for action for my slumber had been accomplished on the softest of feather beds. A family fled from a farmhouse just behind our lines and, as the back door was ajar, I decided to have a look around. Finding the house empty and the featherbed unoccupied, I enjoyed a pleasant night's respite from the hardships of army life.

As I opened my eyes, it was growing light and I realized that General Jackson had probably been up and active for some time. Remembering his insistence on "early risers," I quickly pulled on my boots, the only article other than my belt and holster that I had removed before retiring. Suddenly, the whole house shook and roared and I was enveloped in a gray cloud that issued forth from the fireplace. I scurried outside, spitting and coughing the dust from my throat and lungs.

Looking at the dwelling, it became clear what had happened. A random enemy cannon shot had struck the chimney directly above my second floor bedroom.

Instead of thanking the Almighty for deliverance, I cursed the northern devil who pulled the lanyard on that shot.

Word of this misadventure spread among the staff and brought from General Jackson a short but stern lecture that I should be court-martialed for entering a civilian house without permission. All in all, my night in the featherbed was scarcely worth it.

My breakfast consisted of bread and molasses washed down by a couple of swallows of cold milk from a nearby

spring house. General Jackson soon had me in a flurry running orders all along the line to this Colonel and that Major.
My morning dusting made me quite uncomfortable. Though
the day began with fog and the threat of rain, before long,
the sun burned off the mists. Soon it grew warm and I resolved to find a stream to bathe in at the first opportunity.
That opportunity would not be soon in coming for the great
battle at Pipe Creek was about to begin.

The Union artillery offered a sporadic, desultory fire
which was more annoying than dangerous. With the bombardment, General Meade hoped to draw us out and reveal
more of our position. Most of our army remained concealed
behind ridges and wood lines. For a time, Generals Early
and Ewell speculated that the Yankees might assault us. To
this idea, Jackson growled, "If they do, they will be destroyed."

Now this might seem a curious statement by a general
about to launch a similar assault. But, like Lee, he had every
confidence in his men and had witnessed us triumph time
after time.

Through the early morning, Jackson kept me busy so I
did not notice the hours passing. Yet each time I returned to
the General, he held his watch in hand. By eight o'clock,
Generals Lee and Jackson were obviously concerned over
the delay of Longstreet's attack and Lee sent at least two
messages inquiring as to the reason for the hold-up.

Finally, at eight-thirty, we heard the sounds of battle
toward the west. It would be the C. S. right flank. Both Lee
and Jackson stiffened in the saddle as the sweet and awful
signal reached our ears. Jackson at once gave the order for
our artillery to commence firing and our gunners jumped
into action. General Jackson sent me riding to General Johnson whose division occupied the left of our corps, near the
village of Union Mills.

Johnson was to lead the order of assault. While Longstreet's Corps rolled in on the Union left, Johnson would at-

tack the opposite end of the enemy's line. This would be followed by the successive advances of Early, Ewell, and Rodes. In theory, that would push the Union Army backward, breaking its lines and delivering a magnificent Southern victory.

I found General Johnson in an exposed position, watching the enemy as his troops prepared for the assault. Known as "Old Allegheny" or "Clubby" to the men, Johnson stood by a tree, leaning on his cane. When I gave him General Jackson's order to advance, his face lit up like a child at Christmas.

"This is it, boy. The end of the war," he said as I accompanied him back to where his men waited.

They were magnificent troops and included the Stonewall Brigade with whom General Jackson had earned his reputation at Manassas. There seemed not a tinge of fear, only a tremor of excitement as the ragged butternut ranks fixed bayonets and brought their arms to right shoulder shift.

General Johnson reviewed the line, chattering as he went. "Come on, brave fellows. One more fight then home. I'm going right up there with you. Wouldn't miss it for the world. One more fight and then home."

The flags were uncased and the drums beat the advance. The lines started out at route step, stretched across the summer fields, and moved into sight of the Union position. General Johnson rode with them, still on horseback. It was madness to ride a horse on such an assault yet I, too, found myself being drawn along in their wake.

The enemy fire grew hotter. Artillery blew holes in our lines but the men closed ranks and continued their determined, unhurried pace. We splashed through Pipe Creek, some of the men scooping water as they marched. To my right was the Westminster Road, which crossed up the ridge and passed through the Yankee lines. Ahead stood a red brick mill. I paused behind the mill where it seemed somewhat safe and tied my horse, unwilling to take the animal into certain death. Several skulkers had already sought refuge there and I chased them on with the point of my father's sword. Then I hurried to catch up with the advancing line as we swept past a handsome, wood frame house. Flames could be seen dancing through the roof of the residence and soon it was reduced to ashes.[14]

We hit the Yankee defenses where the road curves across the crest of the hill. The Rebel yell rang instinctively up and down the line as we lost all semblance of order and rushed over their breastworks. General Johnson, now dismounted, scrambled atop a cannon, toppled a Yankee with his walking stick, and then he, too, fell.

Crossing the barricade, I felt a hand on my shoulder and turned to see a headless torso. The unfortunate soul's blood splattered my left side as I broke free and jumped a fence. I emptied my revolver into a blurred mass of blue uniforms and then began swinging the saber. A Yankee pushed at me with a cannon rammer but I dogged the blow and struck him, instead. At my feet was a pistol. I grabbed it, fired the two shots that remained, and then tossed the weapon at the enemy.

This was the moment of our crisis. Had we had another brigade, had we had even another regiment, we could have whipped those fellows of the Fifth Corps who held that line. But there were no reinforcements to be had and the enemy's Sixth Corps was coming to their support. Our brave fellows retreated in bloody disorder through the fields we had just crossed.

I looked behind the mill, but my horse was gone. To the west, Early's men had just hit the enemy line and officers of Johnson's Division were imploring their men to re-form for

---

[14] The Andrew Shriver homestead. Andrew supported the north and owned slaves. His brother, William, supported the south and did not own slaves. William's house was also destroyed during the battle.

another assault. But it was no use. We had done our best and, on that day, our best wasn't good enough. Our losses were severe but not crippling and we knew the army would yet win its victory on the morrow. We returned to our starting position to prepare for an enemy counter-attack.

After a brief rest, I made my way back to General Jackson. Along the way, I watched Early's and Ewell's men return. General Jackson, realizing the failure of the other divisions, halted Rodes' advance shortly after it had begun.

But what of General Longstreet? How had his attack fared? There, too, our plans fell into disarray.

General Longstreet had not given up the idea of a flanking movement and members of his staff had spent the evening searching for a way around the Union left. A route was found but it was blocked by a couple of regiments of Yankee cavalry who were sparring with Imboden's men. An alternative route went across fields partly exposed to the view of the Federals. Longstreet sent a message to General Lee imploring that the flanking movement be reconsidered, using this route.

Lee again rejected the suggestion and repeated his order for an early assault.

That morning, the First Corps prepared for its attack. Artillery was brought into position. Troops formed in line of battle. But the preparations did not go smoothly and Longstreet did not order the advance until long after what he had promised the previous day.

On the Union left, the great Dan Sickles grew nervous over all this Rebel activity. The commander of the Third Corps felt certain that we were about to repeat our Chancellorsville maneuver. There, Sickles had boldly advanced and struck Jackson's Corps during its flank march. With proper support, he might have saved the Federals from defeat. Now Dan Sickles felt sure it was going to happen again.

Sickles rode to and fro, scanning the horizon through his field glasses. Then, shortly after eight-thirty, his vigil was rewarded. He saw the gleam of bayonets as Longstreet's advance began.

Sickles quickly sent one messenger and then another to Meade. He waited and waited and then he waited no longer. He ordered the entire Third Corps to advance upon the enemy.

General Longstreet observed Sickles' advance immediately, later calling it "a grand movement, as if the entire corps was on the parade ground." At the time, "Old Pete" probably had a more colorful description for it. There was no alternative but to deploy his men to meet the enemy. Longstreet's assault was being met with a counter-assault.

Thus began a see-sawing engagement that continued long after Jackson's fight had spent itself. Returning from Johnson's Division, I heard the furious fire raging to the west and wondered if Longstreet was succeeding. Throughout the day, each side kept feeding troops into the fight with only the grim reaper gaining any benefit.

By mid-day, Sickles' Corps had been pretty well chewed up and made its way back to the safety of the main line. During the withdrawal, a shell fragment struck Sickles and his leg was amputated later that evening. Nowadays you can see Dan's limb on display in Washington where the General visits it often.

In Longstreet's Corps, General Barksdale of Mississippi was killed and General Hood of Texas was wounded.[15]

The action on the west end of the field spawned two of the main controversies of the Battle of Pipe Creek.

The first of these is General Longstreet's alleged slowness on the morning of July 3. In an ideal world, General Longstreet should have attacked at dawn -- about the same time I was getting out of bed. But military campaigns don't take place in an ideal world. Students of the war will remember Jackson's tortoise-like movements during the Pen-

---

[15] General Hood won fame leading the Texas Brigade but he was a native of Kentucky.

insula Campaign. Even at Chancellorsville, his flanking movement took an entire day to get into position and the attack ended in confusion with the nightfall.

Yet, some self-appointed guardians of our Confederate history revere Jackson while disparaging Longstreet. They forget that every commander has his share of success and failure; better generals just have more of the former.

In truth, our army attempted to do too much too soon. In the haste to follow up on our victory at Gettysburg, our troops had scarcely arrived on the field before the grand strategy had been decided. The roles of the First and Second Corps were decreed before either of their commanders had made more than a superficial reconnaissance over the ground. Stuart, preoccupied with the enemy's cavalry, was unable to provide his usual, thorough intelligence. Indeed, scouting for the First Corps was done by an engineering officer from Longstreet's staff.

But what of that other controversy, General Sickles' grand advance of the Third Corps?

Here, too, I must support the actions of the corps commander. By boldly advancing, General Sickles stopped Longstreet as his attack was just getting underway, ruining the entire army's battle plan. When Jackson heard the guns and gave Johnson the order to advance, we were not assaulting an army whose other flank was "being rolled up like a blanket" but an army on the alert, ready to strike back.

True, Sickles acted without orders and his men suffered awesome casualties. But, sensing an emergency, an able commander must be willing to accept the risk of his own initiative. As Lincoln said of Grant, "I like the man. He fights." General Sickles, too, was a bully boy who was not afraid to go after the enemy. If I may pay him the highest compliment, General Sickles' performance was more like that of an officer of our army than of his own.

Let us suppose, for a moment, that General Sickles had stayed in place and awaited our attack. Longstreet could then have struck at the point of his own choosing. Perhaps he would have succeeded, perhaps he would have failed. General Meade may even have shifted troops to his left to meet this threat, weakening the line where Jackson struck and allowing our success at that point.

In all this, we are simply playing with the thread of history. We delude ourselves to believe that the end result would have been other than that which was.

So enough speculation! All I know for certain is that, on the awful afternoon of July 3, I was one miserable soldier. I was hot, tired and dirty, my horse had been stolen and I was certain General Jackson would put me under arrest for taking part in Johnson's charge. My proper role was to deliver Jackson's message and return immediately to the General.

On this matter, however, my fears proved groundless. Seeing my return, Jackson merely asked me where I'd been. I told him I had gone along with Johnson. He said quietly, "I thought so" and then turned away. "Old Jack" was not the kind of general to punish a soldier who fights.

And it was not long before I was in another scrap. Walking through the melee of the battle's aftermath, I spied a fat sergeant astride my horse, "Old Abe." This fellow must have been with the commissary department; the rations the average man in our army got were nothing to build a belly like this fellow had.

I marched up to this sergeant and said undiplomatically, "Give me back my horse, you thief."

The fat man told me to proceed to a very hot place and started to ride away. I lunged forward, pulling him from the saddle and onto me. I fell to the ground with the fat man on my back and he began pummeling me. I tried to break free but his weight kept me in place.

Then a stern voice ordered, "Stop that! Have we not enough of those people to fight without fighting among ourselves?"

I looked up to see General Lee. The fat man jumped off me and saluted. I wiped the blood from my nose and blurted, "He stole my horse!"

"I found that horse, General."

Lee looked at me for a long moment and asked, "You are with General Jackson?"

"Yes, sir."

"And this is your horse?"

"Yes, sir."

Lee turned to the fat man, "You found this horse?"

"Yes, sir."

"I believe it belongs to this young man. Return it to him and go back to your duties."

I triumphantly ran to my horse while the fat man waddled away. Still it worried me that every time General Lee saw me, I did something embarrassing.

The armies were now back in their respective positions. Even Longstreet's Corps had broken off fighting and returned to where they started. Our army was again disorganized and I followed Jackson as he moved through his command, barking orders. His eyes burned like coals from beneath the rough brim of his battered forage cap. At any moment, he expected a Federal counter-attack and he was eager for it to come.

But the Federals did not attack. General Meade seemed quite satisfied to leave us alone and this was probably a smart thing to do. For, though bloodied, we were not beaten and any Union assault would have been repelled at great loss.

The question, of course, was what would happen next. Both armies were strongly positioned and each could sit for days, even weeks, waiting for the other to attack. However, the Army of the Potomac sat directly on a rail line which brought more equipment and substance every day. Our army was supplied by a circuitous wagon route which picked up supplies at the railhead in Staunton, brought them through Winchester, over the Potomac, past Hagerstown, and across the mountains to Emmitsburg. Because of that, shipments were erratic and the trains were open to enemy attack. While foodstuffs could be gathered from the countryside, ammunition could not and, already, our artillery chiefs worried about their shrinking supply of shot and shell.

That evening, Generals Lee, Jackson, Longstreet, and Ewell rode the lines and discussed the morrow. Stuart was not present; his plans had been thwarted in a series of thrusts and counter thrusts with the Union horsemen and the cavalier remained on guard against a renewal of the fight.

I did not participate in the evening ride but used the time to recover from the day's adventure. But I learned much of what went on.

General Lee proposed renewing the battle the next day with a direct assault on the center of the Federal line. Longstreet opposed the plan, reiterating his preference to go on the defensive and let Meade attack us. Jackson, as always, was ready to fight. It was decided that Rodes' Division of Jackson's Corps and Pickett's Division of Longstreet's Corps, neither of whom had participated in the battle of July 3, should spearhead the assault.

That evening, it began to rain.

Chapter Seven

JULY 4

On the morning of July 4, the rain had stopped. I accompanied General Jackson to the extreme front of our picket line where, for a very long time, he observed the enemy through his field glasses. He said nothing but I could tell he did not like what he saw. Even without the aid of a glass, it was apparent that the Yankees had spent the night strengthening their works.

Upon our return, we met General Longstreet. Longstreet told us he had also taken a good look at the center of the Federal line and this made him no more sanguine about our prospects. Jackson said he still favored the assault unless a better plan could be developed.

"Well, this is the Fourth," Longstreet replied, "Maybe General Meade will fire a salute come noon and they'll attack us then."

Jackson nodded and the two generals went to Lee's headquarters where it was decided that our assault would be held off until afternoon in the hope that Meade would come to us. If not, our guns would shell the enemy's position in preparation for the charge of Rodes and Pickett.

Noontime found us lunching on pork, beans, and freshbaked bread. The enemy had fired no celebratory cannonade and General Jackson was about to issue orders to our guns when it began to rain once again. I expected that this would have little effect on our battle plans. I had heard the story of an officer complaining at the Battle of Ox Hill that the rain had made our gunpowder wet and Jackson merely replied that the enemy's powder was wet, too.

But, in this instance, the downpour seemed to take on a great significance and Jackson told several of us to mount up and go with him to see General Lee. We huddled on a farmhouse porch while Lee and Jackson met inside. After a time, Longstreet arrived and, soon thereafter, we learned the assault would not take place.

In truth, I believe that General Jackson had increasing doubts about the possibility of success for an attack on the Federal center. But, it was not in his nature to back away from a fight, particularly one that General Lee believed in. The rain gave him an excuse to suggest that the movement not be made.

Looking back, the decision seems to have been the correct one. Under clear skies, perhaps a direct assault could have crushed their center but, in the deluge of that afternoon, it is unlikely to have succeeded. The very heavens seemed to open upon us and mere canvas was no protection. Fields became vast mud holes and Pipe Creek, which separated us from our enemies, grew in size and speed.

I spent the first part of that afternoon exposed to the elements, carrying orders to the division commanders. Afterward, I secreted myself in a spring house where several other staff officers had found shelter. Protected from the elements, I took a nap.

When I awoke, I located General Jackson and General Ewell sitting on the front porch of a house examining one of Jed Hotchkiss' maps. I came as close as possible without intruding upon their conference but, at my approach, General Jackson rose, slapped his hands and said, "Well, that's it! I shall go gather up General Longstreet and together we can see General Lee."

As if by serendipity, Generals Lee and Longstreet appeared down the pike, wrapped in their oilcloths and riding toward us. General Jackson sent me running through the rain to hail them. In their company were two Englishmen, Colonel Fremantle and a fellow named Flashman.

The four generals gathered on the front porch while several of us took our British visitors back to the shed. Colonel Fremantle passed around a silver flask and entertained us with stories of his travels. He had a high opinion of our army and seemed to believe that England somehow deserved part of the credit for our success.

We engaged in a lengthy debate on what the army would do next, no doubt a subject similar to that being discussed on the front porch. The consensus of our group was that we would launch a massive assault against the Yankees come July 5 and drive them back to Washington. But one of the fellows from Ewell's staff was wise in disagreement.

"Oh, I don't know," he drawled. "Old Blue Light don't like to fight on a Sunday so I don't think you'll see any fuss tomorrow."

As it turned out, he was right.

The commanders' conference lasted nearly two hours, after which General Jackson had me running off to find General Johnson. This came as a surprise, for the last I had seen of "Old Allegheny" was when he had fallen during the previous day's assault on the Federal right. As it happened, he had merely been stunned, temporarily taken prisoner, and, in the post-battle confusion, had made his way back to our lines. After a night's rest, he resumed command of his division.

Nevertheless, he was quite a spectacle. A huge bandage encircled his head, making it impossible to wear a hat. The front of his coat was badly ripped and dark blood stains dotted the gray cloth. He leaned heavily on his club with one hand and held the remnants of a black umbrella above his head with the other. Even in our army, which was not noted for sartorial splendor, this get-up stood out.

I handed him the note from General Jackson. He read it immediately and exclaimed, "I do believe he's lost his mind, sir! I do believe General Jackson has lost his mind."

He called for his horse and insisted I take him to the corps commander. On the ride back, he spoke to me as if I knew the contents of the message, which I did not.

"For us to pull our troops out of line and march through this flood is impossible. Maybe if we had an ark. Has General Jackson built an ark, sir? Is that what this is all about? Why do we not stay and fight?"

To none of this could I respond and it was with relief that I saw General Jackson still on the front porch. He and General Johnson had an animated discussion, though, in the middle of it, I was sent off with orders to an artillery unit. During my ride, I puzzled the meaning of Johnson's protest about marching in this weather.

In the middle of this, my horse threw a shoe and it was with much difficulty that I found a blacksmith and had it repaired. Returning to headquarters, Lieutenant Morrison warned me, "Better get a good night's sleep. It's going to be a long day tomorrow."[16]

That turned out to be an understatement.

Jim woke me well before daybreak. General Jackson was already up and Johnson's Division passed by on the road. The rain continued and, even through my sleepy eyes, it was evident that the troops marched with great difficulty in the sea of mud. Around the camp fire, I drank a cup of coffee and General Jackson announced that we would march toward Emmitsburg and that we must keep the troops closed up. He said nothing more and we knew it would be fruitless to ask.

General Johnson rode up and announced that his entire division was underway, to which General Jackson grunted, "Good."

"This will be a difficult march, General."

"Then it will be just as difficult for the enemy to follow us," Jackson replied.

---

[16] Joseph G. Morrison was Jackson's brother-in-law.

I mounted "Old Abe" and followed General Jackson's sorrel. I wondered if we were retreating or if we were advancing back into Pennsylvania. Whatever, I trusted that the genius of Stonewall Jackson would make everything come out all right.

And it was a tremendously difficult march. The rain continued into the daylight and wagons and cannons frequently became stuck. The roadway seemed to be nothing but a bottomless pit of mud and many a poor soldier lost his shoes in the mire. To make matters worse, General Imboden's cavalry had preceded us, escorting a wagon train of wounded back to Virginia. Their passage cut up the roadway, making our progress even more difficult.

Among the soldiers, little grumbling took place. They, too, trusted that Old Stonewall would not make them endure this without reason and that the payoff would be another brilliant victory over the Yankees.

The proof of this came as we turned left before reaching Emmitsburg. The column was not retreating over the mountains; we were making a wide flank march to get between the enemy and Washington. A cheer went up and down the ranks; General Jackson ordered us to hush the troops for fear of revealing our intentions.

A student of the war may be interested in how that decision had been made. Surely, given the condition of the roads, the logical course would have been for our army to remain in place and slug it out. But General Jackson's victories were not built on what was logical and, as I have indicated earlier, I believe he became less enthusiastic about our chances for victory in a direct frontal assault. Studying his maps, he reasoned that, by swinging wide to the west, he could skirt Meade's army and gain a position around Frederick. This would make Meade's Pipe Creek line untenable, forcing a withdrawal to protect Washington. In achieving that, Meade would open himself to defeat. Even if the Army of the Potomac made it back to Washington's defenses, Baltimore would be exposed to capture and Washington itself would soon follow.

This strategy relied on several factors. The first was that the march could be made in a reasonable time, given the condition of the roads. Here, General Jackson had no doubt that his men could accomplish what he asked. The second was that the Union Army would remain in place behind Pipe Creek, awaiting our attack. The third was that, for a while, at least, General Longstreet could hold off any Federal assault.[17]

In their front porch conference, Longstreet asserted he could defend his line "until Pipe Creek freezes over." Jackson assured him that would be far longer than required. Lee remained uncertain of the flanking maneuver, preferring the direct assault, but, after discussion, he yielded to his lieutenants.

No student of the war should find this daring strategy surprising. Had Lee not split his army during the campaigns of Second Manassas and Sharpsburg? At Chancellorsville, Lee faced Hooker's army with only two divisions while Jackson made his flank march. By comparison, the current strategy looked positively safe.

In the event the Federals attacked and Longstreet was forced to withdraw, he could do so through the Emmitsburg gaps which offered ideal defensive positions. Jackson, on the other hand, could retire to Fox's Gap and Turner's Gap, west of Frederick, if confronted by an overwhelming force. Stuart was to remain on the army's left, screening any Federal flanking maneuver. A brigade of cavalry under "Grumble" Jones accompanied Jackson to provide reconnaissance.

I met General Jones for the first time on that terrible march. He was a profane old man who reminded me of

---

[17] The commanders briefly considered a march by Jackson to the east around the Union right flank toward the Westminster railroad. This was rejected for, if disaster had struck, Jackson would have had no open line of retreat back to Virginia. Longstreet volunteered to make the march around the Union left, but such a move would have required repositioning the entire army.

General Early and, at each meeting, I approached him with caution. He'd fought Indians on the frontier before the war and, though he's been eclipsed by the colorful Stuart and Hampton, I believe Jones was one of our best cavalry leaders. Only the day before, he virtually destroyed the Sixth United States Cavalry as that unit tried to get to our supply trains at Emmitsburg. Before me, I have General Jones' report of that affair in which he succinctly states "the Sixth U.S. Regular Cavalry is now among the things that were."

We did not go far on the Frederick Road before we ran into the enemy's horsemen. The bluecoats would deploy along a ridge or fence line, fire a few volleys into our advance, and then be gone before we could catch them. Generally, our cavalry kept the way clear but, several times, our infantry had to stop and fan out into a line of battle. The Yankee cavalry caused little damage, but they did delay us and add annoyance to an already unpleasant procession.

In general, the Frederick Road was in better shape than the one we started out on for we no longer followed our ambulance trains. Jackson even left most of our wagons behind to speed the march.

Nevertheless, in short order, the Frederick Road became a difficult passage. Several times, I pitched in alongside General Jackson to help free a stuck cannon or wagon. On one occasion, I fell full-face into the mud and, for the remainder of the march, would have been a contender for the dirtiest Rebel in Lee's Army.

At Mechanicstown, Jackson turned Ewell and Johnson's Divisions southeast toward the village of Liberty Town, placing them in position for an assault on the Union left and rear.[18] Early's Division continued to Frederick to confront an enemy force that our scouts reported near that place.

Jackson allowed us ten minutes' rest each hour but this was small comfort given the traveling conditions. At one

---

[18] Now Thurmont, Maryland.

o'clock, the column halted for two hours and some of the men attempted to build fires to cook over. Most of us, including myself, had already finished whatever rations we carried in our haversacks. At three o'clock, we resumed the march.

Toward evening, a messenger arrived from General Early and reported that part of the Union Army's VIII Corps under General French was at Frederick.

Early's note also said prisoners reported that our pontoon bridge across the Potomac at Williamsport had been destroyed. We refused to believe our lifeline to Virginia was severed and put the story down as a Yankee lie. Later, to our dismay, we discovered the truth of their statement.

At this point, dear reader, put yourself in the place of General Jackson. You have offered a bold and daring plan to divide the army in the face of the enemy and your superior officer has accepted this plan with some reservation. Your troops have marched through terrible conditions with little rest or food. You find yourself in an advanced position, exposed to the enemy on all fronts with little prospect of supply or assistance. And, now, having split your force into two parts, you learn that an enemy of unknown strength is just a short march behind you.

It is a mark of Jackson's greatness that at no time did he sink into doubt or despair. Like all great commanders, he kept his eye up the key to victory and moved resolutely toward it. History must also record that the men of his command did not fail beneath their fatigue and hunger but obeyed their general's orders as if they had been freshly rested and fed.

Jackson scribbled an order and handed it to Early's courier. Then he said to me, "Go with him and come back when General Early has driven the enemy." I saluted and we rode off across the fields.

Our trip involved some risky business, for my companion was scarcely more familiar with the Maryland countryside than I was. Several times we nearly blundered into the enemy and we were shot at on three occasions, twice by the Federals and once by our own soldiers.

As we met General Early, we found that his men had already advanced in line of battle. Our artillery was booming away, though it seemed that as many of the shots exploded over our own men as reached the enemy; General Early ordered them to cease fire.

The Federals let loose several volleys but began to retreat before things got interesting. General Early mounted and rode forward, waving his hat and yelling, "Come on, fellows. Let's catch 'em all. Let's get all the Yankee s___ of b____s!"

Alas, they were too quick for us. Except for a broken-down cannon or two, they got away clean. It is my experience that nothing can move faster than a Yankee on the run--unless, of course, it is a Rebel in the same situation.

Some of our more enthusiastic boys pursued French to the outskirts of Frederick. As darkness fell, Early's Division slept where it stopped along the Frederick Road. I made a weary ride back to General Jackson, whom I found near Liberty Town and to whom I reported that French's Yankees were in full retreat.

Jackson merely nodded when presented with these glad tidings. It was as if he'd been told the sky was blue instead of the news that the enemy behind him was no longer a threat.

After taking care of my mount, I walked over to the campfire kettle and helped myself to the badly burnt dregs of something that had once masqueraded as stew. I was trying my best to choke this down when Jackson sat down on the log next to me.

"Randolph, are you ever afraid in battle?" he asked.

I swallowed a mouthful of the awful gruel and quickly pondered whether the General thought I was a coward. Before I could answer, he continued.

"I am never afraid for I know that the Lord has planned all things for the best. I am as safe on the front lines as I am at home in my bed in Lexington."

"Do you really believe that, General?"

"Yes, Randolph. I do." Then Jackson rose and walked off into the darkness.

Chapter Eight

JULY 6

On Monday morning, General Jackson wrote the following message to General Lee, which appears here from the
Official Records:

Monday, July 6
Hdqs., Second Corps
A.N.V.
Near Liberty, Md.

General,
* Our troops entered Frederick City this morning*
after some resistance from the Harper's Ferry
Garrison under General French. Our scouts tell us
that French has taken a position near Monocacy
Junction and I have directed General Early to drive
them from that point. The remainder of my force is
near the village of Liberty Town and ready to
engage General Meade as opportunity dictates.
* Prisoners report the destruction of our pontoon*
bridge at Williamsport but I can not confirm the
truth of their statements.

Yr. obedient servant,
T.J. Jackson
Lt. General

Jackson folded the paper and handed it not to me but to
another courier for delivery. I was disappointed at not being
given such an important errand but felt relief that I would
not have to make the muddy ride back to Taneytown. As it

turned out, our courier got captured by Yankee cavalry under the command of Captain Dahlgren who spirited the note to General Meade. General Lee did not learn of our successful march until later.[19]

General Jackson dispatched me to collect the latest newspapers and, with some difficulty, this was accomplished. These made for amusing reading, filled as they were with accounts of Stuart's capture of Harrisburg and the Yankee defeat at Gettysburg. *The New York Herald* of July 3 contained a large map of the area and a story which said "results of the fighting were not quite clear." I read this aloud and it brought much laughter from those present; through the end of the campaign, any time there was a misfortune or accident, one of the staff would offer up that the "results were not quite clear."

As we sat reading these newspapers, the provost guard brought before us a bearded Scotsman who gave his name as Alexander Gardner, a photographic artist of war scenes. Gardner said he was en route to the battlefront and requested permission to take a likeness of Jackson. This request was refused. When Gardner persisted, Jackson threatened to place him under arrest as a spy and confiscate his wagonload of equipment. Several members of the staff felt this was a wise course under any circumstance. The last I saw of Mr. Gardner, a couple of "Grumble" Jones' cavalrymen were "requisitioning" his horses.

At about eight o'clock, faint echoes of artillery fire came from the northeast. General Jackson correctly assumed that Lee and Meade were fighting along the Pipe Creek line. This caused the greatest anxiety, for we had hoped that our movement would force General Meade's withdrawal and that we could bring him to battle in a position of our choosing. General Jackson pondered the situation and decided he must advance immediately upon the rear of the Union

---

[19] Captain Ulric Dahlgren, who, later in the campaign, lost a leg after being wounded in Hagerstown.

Army. He then took out his silver pencil and scribbled a note which he asked me to carry to General Early in Frederick. I mounted and headed down the road that I hoped would take me to that city.

Nearing the outskirts of town, I encountered some of our pickets who directed me to Early. A lively exchange of cannon fire suddenly filled the air and, before long, I spied the hunched form of "Old Jube" sitting on a fence rail, talking with General "Extra Billy" Smith.

General Smith's true calling was that of a politician and, as I was watching him, it was obvious that he preferred giving orders to taking them. He left the army soon afterward and became Governor of Virginia. He never much liked General Early and General Early never much liked him. Earlier in the invasion, General Early had bawled out "Extra Billy" for halting his troops in York, Pennsylvania, in order to make one of his windy speeches to the local residents.

I handed Jackson's note to "Old Jube" and waited for his reply, which I expected to be caustic and salty. Instead, he got off his fence rail, put his arm around me and pointed to the south.

"Son, General Gordon just crossed the river over yonder and, if you wait a spell, you'll see the Yankees run. Isn't that right, General Smith?"

"Sir, they won't stop until they get to Abe Lincoln's bedroom. They won't stop until that Black Republican has received his just desserts."

"Well, I doubt if 'Old Abe' is there to greet them," Early drawled. "I expect he's skedaddling about now."

At that, our artillery opened with renewed vigor and "Extra Billy" excused himself. General Early gave me his field glasses and I could see the entire Yankee line on the opposite bank of the Monocacy River. Both a covered bridge, which had been destroyed, and an iron railroad bridge, which remained intact, spanned the stream. A few Yankee skirmishers could be seen on our side of the river but most were retreating across the remaining bridge.

I could not see Gordon's men when they first began their assault, although their Rebel yells cut through the noise of our artillery. General Early jerked his glasses from my hand and studied the scene, exclaiming, "Good! Good!" every so often.

As we watched, "Extra Billy" led his soldiers into the fray and soon the Yankee line dissolved. General French had no more heart for fighting that day than he'd had the night before. No doubt French thought he faced the entire Second Corps of the Army of Northern Virginia. Under such circumstance, the fortifications of Washington seemed far more appealing than the banks of the Monocacy.

"If our cavalry was where it should have been, we'd have bagged them all," General Early said.

"I could march the whole way to the White House if I wanted to. But I reckon Jackson'd rather have us fight General Meade. Well, you tell Jackson I'll let Smith chase the Yanks long enough for a good scare. Everyone else will start back directly."

I saluted and returned to Frederick, leaving behind me another of the war's many controversies. To this day, General Early insists, in frequent speeches and voluminous writings, that he could have captured the northern capital had he been allowed to do so. This is so much folly. The Washington defenses were adequate to hold Early's Division until reinforcements arrived. Indeed, the Yankee railroad wizard, General Haupt, had already collected enough rolling stock to move an entire corps back to Washington by rail if need be.

Perhaps the specious nature of Early's claim is most revealed by his blaming of Longstreet for our withdrawal after the victory at Monocacy Junction. According to Early, Longstreet failed by not holding Meade in check at Pipe Creek. This argument ignores the fact that General Lee was in overall command at Pipe Creek and that it was Jackson's decision to withdraw Early. Of course, the politics of our post-war era prevent General Early from acknowledging these facts.

Before returning to General Jackson, I stopped in Frederick and had an excellent meal of flapjacks and sausage. This I paid for with Confederate money which was cheerfully accepted.

Meanwhile, General Jackson had put his remaining two divisions in motion. Ewell and Johnson left Liberty on the road running east. This would take them directly into Westminster, the base of supply for Meade's entire army. What we did not know was that General Meade had put part of his own army in motion.

Observing our departure on the morning of July 5, General Meade called his corps commanders into a council of war where opinions were solicited as to what Lee's army was up to. The responses ranged from a full retreat to a flanking movement to an advance on Pittsburgh![20]

The question then turned to what action the Army of the Potomac should take. Most present stated that the army should hold its position and await developments. However, Generals Hancock and Pleasanton urged an immediate assault upon the part of the Confederate army which remained in place. To this Meade reportedly replied, "If General Lee is in retreat, we have done well enough."

Thus, the old saying that councils of war never fight proved true. Meade sat inactive as Jackson made his long swing around the Army of the Potomac. However, cavalry reports received throughout the day finally convinced Meade that a flanking movement was underway.

That evening, he directed General Sedgwick to take the Sixth Corps, advance toward Frederick and engage any Con-

---

[20] Governor Curtain, of Pennsylvania, believed this to be the case and sent at least three messages to Washington demanding that city be reinforced. Secretary of War Stanton finally fired back an angry telegram saying his excellency should go dig trenches in Pittsburgh if he wishes but quit bothering the War Department about it.

federate force he might find. Meade also drafted orders for an assault to "feel out" the Confederate line at Taneytown. These orders were not issued until the next morning, even though they called for the assault to begin at sunrise.

Lastly, General Meade instructed General Haupt to gather "a sufficient number of cars so as to transport an adequate number of troops by rail for a satisfactory defense of the capital, should the need arise." In addition, Haupt was to "make plans for the destruction of supplies and material gathered at Westminster to prevent such supplies and material from falling into the hands of the enemy."

General Lee had chafed beneath inaction since Jackson's departure the day before. He frequently rode the shortened position held by his remaining soldiers and studied Meade's line for any hint of offense action. He grew increasingly restive over the lack of any communication from his missing corps commander, often asking staff officers, "Have you heard from Jackson? Do we know where he is?"

With the dawn of July 6, Lee's fighting spirit could wait no longer. Concerned that Meade would take the advantage that day, Lee ordered a demonstration by Rodes against the Army of the Potomac's left flank. This was the battle noise Jackson heard while at Liberty Town. Results of the action were inconsequential, except they disrupted Meade's plans to "feel out" the Confederate line. Then the Pipe Creek battlefield again fell quiet.

In the meantime, Ewell and Johnson began their advance upon the Yankee supply base at Westminster. The march had scarcely gotten underway before they encountered skirmishers of the Union Army's Sixth Corps. Johnson deployed his men to the left of the roadway, Ewell to the right, and a sharp engagement commenced.

About this time, I returned from Monocacy and found General Jackson and several officers sitting under an apple tree in view of Sedgwick's sharpshooters. I boldly suggested that the General might retire to a less exposed position but he waved a gloved hand and said, "I don't suppose there's much danger here."

At that, a major from a Carolina regiment pitched forward and fell dead in front of Jackson. The major wore a gaudy uniform with lots of braid and a bright sash. The Yankees probably thought he was the ranking officer of the group. After a few more tense moments, during which another man was hit, Jackson retired to a safer spot and each member of his staff breathed easier.

For the first time, Jackson seemed to lack his usual fire in battle. Fatigue lined his face and dark circles were evident beneath his eyes. I wondered how much sleep he had enjoyed over the past several days or even the past few weeks.

He gave no orders at this moment of crisis and seemed content for events to unfold as they would. When an officer of Johnson's Division appeared and asked for orders, Jackson merely replied, "Drive them, sir. Drive them into the river."

This in itself was a curious statement, for the Monocacy River was behind us and not behind the enemy.

Regardless, this off-hand remark started Johnson's Division forward. The drums rolled and the ragged lines of butternut and gray moved off in route step. The Rebel yell pierced the air as the enemy's guns opened upon our boys and many fell to rise no more.

General Jackson then turned to me and asked, "Is Ewell in position? Has he advanced?"

I replied that I did not know. Then Sandie Pendleton interjected, "You have given General Ewell no orders to advance."

Jackson said irritably, "A soldier does not need orders to fight the enemy. Tell General Ewell to advance."

I rode off and found General Ewell much agitated. His speech fell into a lisp as he gave the order for his brigadiers to go forward. The effect would have been comical had the situation not been so serious.

The battle broke in an open farming countryside which was dotted by occasional rolling ridges and patches of woodland. Neither side had an advantage of terrain, although our foes, being on the defensive, enjoyed a less exposed position.

I stayed with General Ewell and watched the fighting, which gradually drew the old soldier closer and closer to the front. Then I heard a loud thunk and turned, expecting to see General Ewell wounded. To my relief, he was still upright in the saddle and casually remarked, "That's the second time in this campaign I've been shot in my wooden leg."

The battle seesawed back and forth. At one point, we overran a Yankee battery and started to remove the guns but the bluecoats counter charged and took them back. This much disgusted General Ewell. He cursed in his peculiar lisp and then sent me off with a message for General Jackson.

As I rode across the field and through a tree line, I saw a blue column coming directly toward me. I looked around to see if I had strayed off course. Ahead stood Johnson's men. Behind were Ewell's men. It dawned on me that there was a gap in our front, created as the two divisions had advanced. Now the Yankees were moving into the hole and would shortly split our line.

I spurred "Old Abe" who sensed the emergency and soon brought me to General Jackson.

"General, I fear the Yankees have gotten through!"

Jackson replied absent-mindedly, "Randolph, never take counsel of your fears."

"No, General! There's a gap in our lines!"

This time the General listened and sent Sandie Pendleton to take a look but, as Sandie mounted, another officer yelled, "Look! Here come the Yankees now!"

Indeed, they were no more than a few hundred yards from capturing "Stonewall" Jackson. Our party retreated in haste while, without ceremony, enemy bullets were singing around our heads.

Major General Ambrose Powell Hill

The Federal breakthrough neatly divided our position and the bluecoats advanced rapidly to make the most of their advantage. A single artillery battery, for a time, slowed its advance but soon both Ewell and Johnson's Divisions were in retreat. Our troops did not panic but neither did they tarry unnecessarily. Jackson rode among them, thundering orders to stop and face the enemy. I soundly applied the flat of my father's sword to the back of one fellow skedaddling to the rear.

Then, as the situation was at its darkest, General Jackson's face lit up. He smiled and pointed, "Look! It's the Light Division. Tell A. P. Hill to prepare for action."

Jackson, of course, was mistaken. A. P. Hill was two months in a hero's grave. Instead, General Early had returned from his fight at Monocacy Station, and, like A. P. Hill at Sharpsburg, his timely arrival would save us from disaster.

These troops advanced magnificently, banners waving above the solid ranks of gray and butternut. General Gordon could be seen in their front, astride a black stallion and flashing his sword like a god of war. They leveled their bayonets and, once more that afternoon, the Rebel yell ripped through the humid summer air. Every man present knew our crisis had passed.

The blue and gray lines collided like two great violent waves, then each receded to its respective shore. The old Second Corps of the Army of Northern Virginia would not gain the victory we had hoped for that day, but neither would we be driven from the field.

During that battle, I killed a Yankee who had nearly killed me. He was one of several cut off from the main body and I rode toward him, pointed my revolver, and yelled, "Surrender!" He turned with a start and blindly fired a boot pistol at me. The shot tore my jacket, but did no other harm. I fired back and the Yankee roared in pain and rolled over dead.

As the fighting to our front quieted, we could hear that the action along Pipe Creek had resumed. At this, General Jackson began stroking his beard, contemplating what further movement we could take to aid General Lee. It was now early evening with enough daylight left for an attack. But, for once, Jackson saw no opportunity. Our fighting ended except for occasional skirmishes, which killed many a man just as dead as the war's grandest battles.

After dark, I joined General Jackson around the campfire. He was quieter than usual that evening and seemed to be asleep, rousing himself only to eat a little of the beans and bacon which Jim offered. At one point, he began to snore loudly, until he shook himself awake and declared, "Tomorrow we will drive them into the river!" Then he resumed snoring.

Some hours past midnight, when we had all entered into the land of nod, a courier arrived with a dispatch from General Lee, the first we had heard from him since leaving Taneytown.

General Jackson received the message in a bleary-eyed state but the contents immediately awoke him.

Headquarters
Army of Northern Virginia
Taneytown, Maryland
July 6. 1863; 8:00 p.m.

General:

In the late afternoon of this day, General Longstreet made an extensive assault upon the enemy but the enemy's numbers were so great and the position so well prepared that our troops were forced to relinquish their advantage and retire. The enemy suffered severely but our own loss has not been light.

It was my hope that this assault would coordinate with that of your command and bring about a favorable result but this does not appear to be the case.

I believe further assaults upon their line will bring no benefit to our army. No communication has been received from you since your departure but there is no indication your movement has achieved the hoped for results.

You should withdraw as your position dictates to either the mountain passes near Frederick or immediately rejoin our army near Emmitsburg. As I believe the former is the more likely case, you should hold the gaps and prevent the enemy's passage toward Hagerstown and Williamsport.

Should, for some reason, these orders not be practical, I must hear from you at the earliest opportunity. Use extreme prudence for the enemy's cavalry is very active and successful in interrupting our lines of communication.

Very respectfully,
your obt servt,
R.E. Lee
General

Jackson, of course, did not allow us to read this order. Instead, he sent me off to find General Early while two others went to get Ewell and Johnson. Despite the hour, I found Early awake and fully dressed, sitting before his campfire with a cup of something; we returned to Jackson at once.

His officers assembled, Jackson made no mention of General Lee's dispatch. He simply gave orders for a withdrawal through Frederick, commencing immediately. Early's Division would lead, followed by Johnson and then Ewell. The three generals asked a few questions on the route and order of march but no one questioned its why or wherefore. All three were accustomed to -- if not entirely happy with -- Jackson's secretive method of operation and had long ago resigned themselves to their captain's code of silence.

"Grumble" Jones, whose cavalry was to screen our withdrawal, did not remain so silent. The old Indian fighter had arrived late at the meeting and strode about asking anyone, "Why the devil are we going to retreat? There's hell to pay if we do. What's happened that we're going to retreat?"

To this, no one answered. But it was not long before the rumor spread in the ranks that Longstreet had met some terrible reverse at Taneytown and must now be saved. This gave the march an air of somber urgency.

As the meeting broke up, I noticed the first fingers of dawn creeping across the eastern skyline and I put aside any hope of enjoying an additional hour's sleep. The new day had begun.

Chapter Nine

JULY 7

Our withdrawal toward Frederick took place in an orderly fashion. Except for frequent annoyance from its cavalry, the enemy pursued us gingerly and spent much of the day skirmishing with our rear guard on the outskirts of Liberty Town.

It has always been my impression that General Sedgwick was under orders not to pursue us. The reason for this cannot be easily explained. By now, General Meade had to be fully aware that our army was widely separated and he had only to follow through his advantage to realize great benefit.

But General Meade continued his passive campaigning; he was not eager to risk his draw for the chance of a great victory.

This suited us well enough for we had our own problems. Moving toward the South Mountain passes would separate us even farther from the other half of our army. General Lee would cross the mountains at Emmitsburg on the Pennsylvania line; he did this to protect our trains and wounded and to prevent being cut off if he moved south while still east of the mountains.

The Second Corps had its own special set of miseries that day. To expedite our flanking movement, most of the corps' wagons and baggage had been left at Emmitsburg. This resulted in innumerable inconveniences large and small, which grew as the days went on. It also meant that many of our wounded, who could have been otherwise removed from the field, fell into enemy's hands.

In addition, our artillery caissons were dangerously short of ammunition and we had no immediate hope of re-supply. The destruction of our pontoon boats at William-sport and the heavy rains of previous days had severed our connection to Virginia.

Rations were yet another problem, most of the men having long ago consumed the scanty fare with which they had started the march. An unannounced policy of liberal foraging came into effect even though we considered Mary-land to be a sister state of the Confederacy. This slowed our progress and frustrated Jackson, who threatened to shoot anyone he saw engaged in foraging. Nevertheless, the prac-tice continued, for hungry men cannot be stopped from seeking food.

We entered Frederick City and Jackson briefly set up headquarters at the court house. A stout, prosperous-looking individual approached Jackson and introduced him-self as having met the general the previous fall during the Sharpsburg campaign. Jackson nodded and tried to smile but admitted that he had no memory of the man.

"Well, I have great admiration for you, General Jackson, and, as a token of my esteem, I should like to present you with one of the finest horses from my stables if you would only be so kind as to step outside and accept my gift," the fellow said.

This struck several of us as humorous in view of the widespread "requisitioning" of horses that had taken place in the past weeks. But we all adjourned to the street to watch.

The animal was a magnificent beast and looked much like General Lee's "Traveller." Jackson took the reins, ex-pressed his thanks but, despite his benefactor's urging, re-fused to mount the animal. Finally, after requesting an auto-graph with which the General obliged him, the stout man departed. Jackson immediately turned the horse over to Jim.

One of the boys asked Jackson why he had shown so little interest in such a fine steed.

"I am not one to repeat a mistake," Jackson replied. "Last fall, when we were in Maryland, someone else gave me a horse. I mounted it and was thrown. This left me much in pain and, for a time, I was unable to ride. I refuse to chance that again with an unfamiliar animal."

This business completed, I slipped away from Jackson and celebrated my birthday with a meal of flapjacks and syrup.

Our army continued its march through the day, passing over the Catoctin Mountains, and eventually, taking a position astride the South Mountain passes. The natural strength of the line was such that we believed we could hold the position indefinitely against the entire enemy army. Despite the rain, which commenced again that evening, our soldiers worked in the darkness to make our fortress even stronger.

Jackson established his headquarters in a tent alongside the old National Road near the Mountain House. Here we received another communication from General Lee. He had successfully withdrawn from the Pipe Creek position and Longstreet was moving through the mountains en route to Hagerstown. Rodes' Division served as the rear guard. This assignment brought grumblings from some who said that the Second Corps was expected to do all the fighting. Of course, such complaints were groundless for the First Corps had been badly bloodied the previous day and at several other times during the campaign. Soldiers, however, seem to enjoy and even need something about which they can bellyache.

That evening General Jackson drafted a message for General Lee:

July 7
10:30 p.m.

General:

The Second Corps reached the South Mountain passes this evening. Our movement had little interference from the enemy, though they skirmished with our rear guard as it was leaving Frederick City.

Our position is a strong one and, given sufficient ammunition and support, we can hold here to await your orders.

Can you return Rodes to me?

Respectfully,
T.J. Jackson
Lt. General

You can imagine my surprise when General Jackson folded the paper, turned to me, and said, "Take this to General Lee."

Now this was a great honor as I had never been trusted with taking a message to the commanding general. It was also a dubious honor, for it meant a long ride in the rainy darkness after what had already been a full day's march.

But orders were orders, so I got my fresh horse and went off down the muddy western slope of South Mountain, knowing only that General Lee was somewhere to the north on his way to Hagerstown.

Dear reader, I am reluctant to confess this for surely you will wonder about my performance as a courier. Still, truth be told, I fell asleep in the saddle, my horse kept going, and, when I awoke, I knew not where I was except out in the dark and lonely countryside.

I lit a match and looked at my pocket watch but the timepiece had not been wound in several days so it gave the dubious reading of six o'clock. My pocket map offered no clue as to my location, either, and I determined just to continue to ride ahead and see what I should see.

Before long, signs of civilization came into view and I entered a darkened village. I drew my pistol and looked carefully about for a sign of where I was.

"Hello, soldier," a voice called. I whirled in the saddle to see a curious old fellow standing in the shadows beside a hound dog.

"If you're running away, you'd better not go there. You'll run smack into some guards a couple miles down the road."

"I'm not running away. Whose soldiers are down there?"

The old fellow played coy, "Well I dunno. Whose soldiers are you looking for?"

I leveled my pistol at the old man. "I am a Confederate soldier on the staff of General Jackson and, if you don't tell me where I am, I shall shoot you this instant."

The old man's attitude abruptly changed and he quickly informed me that this was the village of Rohrersville. I had gone several miles in the wrong direction. I thanked the old man and asked him why he was up at such an odd hour.

"Can't sleep. Too much going on. Every time you fellows come around there's trouble."

He proceeded to relate his experiences with both armies during the previous year's Sharpsburg campaign but I cut him short, offering the hope that he would have no trouble through the upcoming fighting.

I rode 'til dawn, passing through Boonsboro and quickly covering the fifteen miles to Hagerstown. The journey was uneventful until Funkstown, where a party of the enemy's cavalry blocked the road. In fact, they very nearly captured me for, in the dim light of dawn, it was difficult to distinguish their uniforms. But my horse was quicker than their worn nags, and I galloped off to safety.

Even at this early hour, the streets of Hagerstown bustled with the elements of our army. After a long and unpleasant night's ride, our soldiers were a welcome sight but they looked badly handled to me and I began to wonder about the dimensions of our defeat at Pipe Creek. Such doubts disappeared when I found General Lee. He had been awake for some time and was standing before his tent, sipping a cup of coffee. His person and his uniform were neat and clean and his manner was calm and confident. I briefly wondered if he had just spent the night at a nice hotel but, of course, he had not. General Lee seemed to be the only man in our army who was not worn, dirty and tired from the rigors of the past few days even though he had spared himself from none of its exertions.

I presented the dispatch to him and he gave me a kindly smile. "Ah, it's good to hear from General Jackson. I have missed him often over the past few days." Then he offered me a cup of coffee which was the best I'd ever tasted and, from that moment on, I became addicted to the bean.

General Lee directed me to get some sleep but to report to him before I returned to General Jackson. After giving my horse a good feed, I curled up in one of the headquarters wagons and drifted into dreams.

At about noon, I awoke with a start as the wagon jolted down the road. I yelled to the driver to stop but he would have none of it and continued merrily along his bumpy route. I gathered my belongings and unceremoniously decamped from my place of slumber. However, my timing was bad and the jump sent me tumbling into the mud. By now, I was so used to being dirty that this seemed of little consequence. I checked on my horse and then reported back to General Lee, who told me to wait and he would have something for me to take to Jackson in a short while.

I helped myself to a cup of coffee, found a comfortable seat and watched the comings and goings of the army headquarters. After my nap, the soldiers did not seem nearly as bedraggled as before; in fact, everyone seemed quite optimistic about our prospects.

By mid-afternoon, I began to wonder if General Lee had forgotten about me, particularly because he had disappeared for some time. I asked Major Marshall if I could leave and he said, "No, the General wants you to wait."

So, I waited, enjoying a hoecake which was offered me. Finally, in the late afternoon, Major Marshall handed me a dispatch and said, "General Lee would like you to give this to General Jackson."

With that I was off, hoping to make it back up the mountains before darkness fell. Leaving Hagerstown, however, I spied H. B. McClellan of General Stuart's staff entering a private dwelling. Deducing that General Stuart was inside, I decided to pay my respects and inquire of the cavalryman if it was safe to travel my previous route. I did not wish a repeat of my narrow escape of that morning.

I entered the house to find McClellan attempting to rouse Stuart from his slumber on the sofa. This was no small task and, eventually, McClellan took Stuart by the hand and led him, as if sleepwalking, to the dinner table. The hostess, a fine young woman of Southern sympathies, bade me to join their party, since I was, as McClellan had introduced me, "a prominent member of General Jackson's military family."

The meal was delicious but, unlike the rest of us, General Stuart ate sparingly and with great indifference. Finally, our hostess asked if he would like a boiled egg.

Stuart raised his head and said strangely, "Yes, I'd like four or five." Then he sank back into his trance. When the eggs were placed before him, Stuart ate one and retreated to the sofa. We finished the dinner in polite conversation, each of us wondering silently about our cavalry chief's curious behavior.

We adjourned to the piano and began singing, "Jine the Cavalry." This being one of Stuart's favorite airs, he arose and came over to us. McClellan slipped into the kitchen and apologized profusely to our benefactress for his commander's odd behavior.

Stuart's unusual demeanor could only be explained by his utter state of exhaustion. Generally, Stuart had extraordinary reserves of energy, required minimal sleep, and always awoke clear-eyed and ready. This campaign, however, seemed to have overtaxed even his abilities of endurance.

McClellan told me that the enemy's cavalry had pushed across the mountains from Mechanicstown and remained active in the area through which I would be riding.

"Keep a sharp eye and your pistol handy. You'll be all right," he said in a cheery voice that was not comforting. I resolved not to fall asleep on my upcoming ride and, luckily, the journey went without incident. I reached General Jackson's headquarters at Turner's Gap in record time.

The morning of July 9 gave me the first real opportunity to examine our position in daylight. The three divisions at hand were spread over the mountain passes. Johnson and Ewell occupied Turner's Gap and Fox's Gap while Early was off to the south at Crampton's Gap. Later that day, Rodes' Division was returned to us but held in reserve on the western base of the mountain.

The area we occupied had been the scene of heavy fighting during the previous autumn and the scars and debris of battle remained in evidence. One of the boys found a human skull which I examined with a mixture of horror and fascination.

I visited a stone monument which had been built to honor George Washington and which pre-dated the more famous marble obelisk in the Federal capital.

From our perch, the Union Army could be seen massing in the valley below. Our pickets kept up a sporadic fire along the lower reaches of the mountain but Billy Yank had little appetite for a fight that day. Though we yearned for the enemy to come at us in our Gibraltar, we equally enjoyed the luxury of being left unmolested in our mountain retreat. The soldiers spent their hours patching pants, sewing buttons and attending to the housekeeping chores which go neglected during vigorous campaigning.

By mid-day, General Jackson decided that no fighting would take place imminently and asked several members of the staff, including myself, to accompany him to General Lee's headquarters. We proceeded down the mountain into Boonesboro where we encountered General Lee and company en route to see us. Lee expressed a desire to review our position so we followed him back up the mountain.

Jed Hotchkiss set a big, brass telescope upon a tripod and the two generals spent a full hour studying the enemy below. They were joined by Generals Ewell and Johnson, the former somewhat in pain from his artificial leg and the latter's attire somewhat improved since I'd last seen him.

General Longstreet also arrived with his staff and I began to wonder if there were any generals left at Hagerstown with the First Corps.

Longstreet was in an upbeat mood and congratulated Jackson on his "natural fortress."

Jackson replied, "Yes, it is a strong position, but even strong positions can be taken. You recall Chapultepec."

Longstreet nodded. "Yes, I remember very well. I was wounded there. But it was not this army which held Chapultepec and it was not General Jackson who was charged with its defense."

"Had we had sufficient strength here last fall, the campaign would have ended differently," Lee said.

"Do you think Meade will attack?"

"I think General Meade would rather do anything than attack, but he may not have a choice," Lee ruminated.

"We'll await their attack?"

"Yes. We must. The Potomac is still too high to cross but I hope to get some artillery ammunition over here to us soon."

"My chests are nearly empty," Jackson acknowledged.

Lee pointed in the distance. "Those people have to come this way. They cannot cross the mountains to the north and leave Washington exposed. To the south, the river is too high. They have to come here."

"What about Harper's Ferry?"

"They've abandoned it but that does us no good. The bridges are destroyed."

Jackson stared through his field glasses. "I think General Meade will be after us in a day or two. He must have his whole army down there."

"I agree. Our next fight should be here," Longstreet said.

"General Jackson, can you hold this line until General Longstreet is up?"

"I can hold it," Jackson said flatly. "I have sent General Rodes toward Harper's Ferry to cover our right and prevent the enemy from getting behind us."

"Wasn't that Rodes I passed coming here?" Lee asked.

"Part of the division is already underway."

Lee nodded and turned his attention back toward the enemy. He said wistfully, "General Meade must attack us. He cannot just sit there."

An officer came running up the mountain to where Lee stood. He saluted and thrust forward a newspaper.

"We just took this off a Yankee prisoner."

Lee opened the folded newspaper. His face turned almost the color of his uniform and he edged backward. Without comment, he handed the paper to Longstreet who in turn, handed it to Jackson. Over Jackson's shoulder, I could see the masthead of the *Philadelphia Inquirer*. There was a large map and a headline reading "Vicksburg is Ours!"

"We were just talking about Chapultepec," Longstreet said bitterly. "So much for invincible strongholds."

"Our last outpost on the Mississippi is surrendered," Jackson shook his head.

"And an entire army lost."

"This is sad news but we shall recover," Lee said. "We must trust in the wisdom of the Almighty's judgment."

"Indeed," Jackson added.

Lee seemed to reinvigorate himself. "General Longstreet, move a division toward Cavetown to block the mountain pass and keep the enemy's cavalry out. Bring the rest of your troops to fortify this line. I'll hold General Stuart near Hagerstown to handle any threat from that area."

"We'll await General Meade's attack?" Longstreet asked.

"Yes."

"Good!"

"And we can expect artillery ammunition tomorrow?" Jackson asked.

"The flatboat is still crossing at Falling Water. We'll get some over the river and down to you."

With that, the conference broke up. Word of Vicksburg's fall quickly spread and, coupled with our own recent reverses, cast a pall over the army. The troops remained confident, however, that we'd even the score in our next match with Billy Yank.

That evening, being bored, I borrowed a Sharps Rifle and worked my way down to our picket line where there was on-and-off sniping at the enemy. I shot a number of times and got shot at a number of times but my bullets had no more effect than those the bluecoats fired at me. After a while, I returned to camp to enjoy a nice rest.

Chapter Ten

THE SECOND BATTLE OF SOUTH MOUNTAIN

The next morning, General Jackson sat doing paperwork under a tent fly tied between two trees. Every twenty minutes or so, he'd put down his papers, walk forward to scan the enemy's position, and then return to his writing.

Already down the slope of the mountain, the popping of small arms could be heard. It was not enough firing to be called a battle but it certainly could not be confused with a deer hunt.

Though Longstreet had not yet arrived, Jackson eagerly awaited the Federals and hoped they would assault us early in the day. He had every confidence of holding his line.

"I am afraid the leaves will change color before General Meade brings his men after us," he lamented.

General Lee established his headquarters just outside Boonsboro on the western base of the mountain. In fact, however, Lee spent most of his time atop the mountain and seemed just as eager for the Federal to go on the offensive.

Longstreet completed the uncomfortable, thirteen-mile march from Hagerstown shortly after noon, leaving behind, at Cavetown, Hood's old Division, now under the command of Evander Law.

Longstreet's welcome reinforcements presented a logistical problem in this steep and wooded terrain. Johnson's Division of Jackson's Corps was to leave Turner's Gap and march to Crampton's Gap to support Early. McLaws' and Anderson's Divisions of Longstreet's Corps were to take over the position formerly held by Johnson while Longstreet held Pickett's Division in reserve.

All this shuffling had to be accomplished on a roadway that was already clogged with traffic. Even under the best of circumstances, maneuvering troops on the crest of that mountain wilderness would have been difficult; doing so in the face of the enemy was flirting with disaster.

Those troop movements were still underway when the Yankee artillery began its bombardment. General Lee smiled and said, "Well, I was afraid those people were going to keep us waiting up here."

On the pike, a mass of blue could be seen slowly moving forward, as if on a leisurely stroll instead of a deadly assault.

General Jackson crouched on a rock, forage cap pulled low over his eyes, staring intently toward the Sharpsburg Road. The enemy's artillery banged away furiously but our own guns rarely responded.

A captain in a bright red cap approached Jackson and said, "General, our limbers are nearly empty. Have we no ammunition for our artillery?"

Jackson pointed to the captain's sword. "If we have no ammunition, we will give them cold steel. Return to your post and do your duty."

The captain turned toward his guns but, before reaching them, an enemy shell exploded and killed the man. A small fragment from the same explosion struck General Jackson's sword, knocking the weapon from its scabbard and throwing its owner to the ground. Several of the boys helped Jackson to his feet while I retrieved the weapon.

This was the same sword Jackson had carried before the war and the shot had badly mangled the hilt, completely removing the ornate "U.S." from the guard. Jackson left it on the field and, shortly thereafter, the ladies of Winchester presented him with an ornate saber of Southern origin, manufactured by Boyle, Gamble & MacFee, an enterprise with which my uncle was associated.

The battle now began in earnest as the enemy pressed its way up the hill. We easily repulsed their uncoordinated assaults which were probing and careful, more designed to test the strength of our line than to break through it. When the Yankees did rush forward and expose themselves, our boys did deadly work and brought down a good many of them. Our casualties were modest, for nearly everyone had availed himself of some kind of cover.

We took some prisoners and learned that the Second Corps was in our front, now commanded by General William Hayes, for its previous commander, General Hancock, had been wounded during Longstreet's Assault on July 6 at Taneytown.

The fighting continued without result through most of the afternoon. A number of our guns emptied their ammunition chests and General Jackson ordered them to be withdrawn. The Yankees saw this, believed we were retreating, and renewed their assault only to be beaten back again.

General Lee came to Jackson with a dispatch. "We have bad news. The enemy's cavalry has captured and destroyed the artillery ammunition we brought over the river at Falling Water."

"Can we get more across?"

"In time."

This was a severe blow to our hopes for success. While Stuart had fought and beaten a large body of the enemy's horsemen at Funkstown, a smaller group had slipped around him and struck the wagon train. Though Stuart caught and punished that group as well, the damage they inflicted could not be undone.

But even worse news followed. In the deploying of Longstreet's men, an inadvertent gap appeared in our lines just as the Yankees launched an assault. As a result, they gained a foothold on the wooded mountain top which they exploited to its fullest. Longstreet called up his reserves but they failed to be deployed in a timely manner due to the crowded roadway and the difficult terrain.

Through the late afternoon, the Yankees pressed their advantage and their success was aided by confusion and blunders on our part. As darkness fell, Longstreet no longer controlled the mountain crests around Turner's Gap.

Given the serious shortage of artillery ammunition and the enemy success on our left, that evening, Lee ordered a retreat to Williamsport, where our pontoon bridge was being reassembled. The dashed hopes of an easy victory in our "impregnable" position made this one of the saddest marches of the war.

Nevertheless, our engineers prepared an admirable defensive position at Williamsport which was fortunate, for we were fighting with our backs to the raging, unfordable waters of the Potomac.

The Union Army followed us and, for a time, it looked like we might get into a pretty good scrap. But the enemy did not attack and, after dark on the evening of July 13, our army crossed into Virginia. By daylight, the movement was complete except for two divisions near Falling Water.

General Jackson sent me off with orders to hurry them along. I set out across the fields and soon heard the sounds of battle. Pulling rein on my horse, I could see Yankees attacking and I decided to take this information back to Jackson immediately. As a precaution, I drew my pistol from its holster.

Just then, I turned to discover two Yankee cavalrymen pointing their carbines at me.

"Cousin," one of them said, "You better drop that gun if you ever want to see your mammy and pappy again."

Chapter Eleven

AFTER GETTYSBURG

My captors were members of the Sixth Michigan Cavalry which was part of the command of General George
Custer, who gave us so much trouble later in the war. When
they learned I belonged to General Jackson's military family,
I was hauled before their young commander for a brief interview.

Custer's colorful dress exceeded even that of J.E.B. Stuart. He wore a suit of black velvet, generously trimmed with
gold braid and brass buttons. A broad shirt collar turned out
over the jacket and a long, scarlet bandanna hung loosely
around his neck. Like our cavalry, he sported a broad-
brimmed, black hat, one side pinned up with a silver star.
His long hair and mustache reminded me of a blonde ver-
sion of our General Pickett.

Custer asked me several sharp questions on the position
and condition of our army. As he did so, he strode about in
his high-topped cavalry boots and slapped a stick against his
gloved hand. Of our position, I could provide little information, for they were all across the river by now; as to our condition, I offered him an enlarged account of how wonderful
we all felt after our excursion to Pennsylvania. He dismissed
me with a curt gesture.

To give him his due, General Custer was an effective
military man but, as his later actions proved, he was no gen-
tleman on the order of Lee, Jackson, or even Grant. After the

war, when word of his death at Little Big Horn reached Virginia, I did not join in the mourning.[21]

They marched me a mile or so to an open field where other prisoners waited. We spent the night under guard and, the next morning, we tramped into Hagerstown. Not until we reached that place were rations issued, so I was pretty well famished. Never before had hardtack and pork tasted so good.

Confederate prisoners.

In Hagerstown, we spent another night before being loaded on the cars of the Cumberland Valley Railroad and shipped north. The journey made me blue twice over. Each passing mile took me farther and farther from Dixie and many of the sights reminded me of our triumphant march through the same countryside just a few weeks earlier. This was particularly true when we crossed the Susquehanna and arrived at Harrisburg.

Here, a sergeant, whose well-fed appearance offered mute testimony to months of garrison duty, separated several officers and me from the main group. We immediately

---

[21] Randolph does not mention that he and Custer nearly came to blows during a post-war meeting in Washington.

boarded another train which departed that evening for Baltimore. This was a more congenial trip, for not only were we headed south, but we also rode comfortably in actual passenger cars. The rumor spread that we should soon be exchanged, the first of many such stories which raised false hopes throughout the months to come.

The Yankee officer in charge of our little group hailed from Vermont and, unlike many of the prison guards we encountered, had actually seen the elephant. He was a nice enough fellow and treated us with none of the disrespect we later endured. In fact, arriving in Baltimore, he bought us a fine meal at Coleman's Eutaw House with his own purse.

After dining, we were taken to Fort McHenry of "Star Spangled Banner" fame. The fort's history stirred no patriotic fervor in my bosom and I spent most of my time thinking up various escape plans.

During my stay, the Yankees interviewed me several times and asked a great many questions on all aspects of General Jackson's command, personality and habits. These I answered truthfully if my response served no military purpose and vaguely if the information could be of value. On several occasions, I invented colorfully wild stories which they believed most readily. In particular, they enjoyed the detailed account of the African mistress who, I solemnly revealed, accompanied Jackson on every campaign.[22]

My interrogators seemed particularly gullible to a tall tale; in another room, they were grilling a prisoner whom they mistakenly believed to be Longstreet!

After a few days, the Yankees either figured they had exhausted the precious little information I could give them or else decided they had captured the village idiot. They shipped me off to Fort Delaware, just outside the city of Wilmington, on Pea Patch Island in the Delaware River.

---

[22] Randolph's tall tales appeared in the *Baltimore Sun*. Reprinted in Richmond, they caused Jackson much embarrassment.

Life here was overcrowded and unpleasant, though I renewed my acquaintance with a number of officers captured during the recent campaign. Through the first months of my captivity, I was quartered and treated as an officer. Even though I held no commission, the Yankees believed I did, given my exalted position on the staff of "Stonewall."

In October, smallpox broke out on the island and the Yankees moved some of their charges to other locations. They sent me to Point Lookout, Maryland, a prison pen which had opened only a month or two earlier on a sandy peninsula in the Chesapeake Bay.

The camp was not much to look at. It consisted of a rectangular fence about ten feet high which enclosed maybe ten or twelve acres. Inside the stockade were rows of canvas tents and several whitewashed, pine buildings which served as kitchens, dining rooms, hospitals, and so on.

On one end of the enclosure stood the main gate and, on the opposite end, were three smaller gates which faced the Chesapeake Bay. These small gates led to privies, built on piers over the water, which could be used by the prisoners during daylight hours.

I spent nearly an entire year at Point Lookout and, during that time, lost my ability to enjoy the ocean. To this day, I cannot look at a painted seascape without memories of that wretched place coming to mind.

A lengthy discussion of my prison experience goes beyond the scope of this narrative. Suffice it to say that there occurred the only period of my life during which I dined on rat.

Through the spring and summer of 1864, new prisoners arrived almost daily--captured in the great campaign then underway. We grilled the newcomers for any scrap of war news and the camp stood united in the belief that Lee and Jackson would soon dispatch General Grant as they had so many other of Lincoln's minions.

During the day, the Yankees allowed us to swim in the bay. A number of prisoners escaped through that route and, in late July of 1864, I decided to try my luck. Halves of wooden barrels were used as wash tubs and, one day, some of the boys hauled one out to the beach. Toward dark, just before the gates closed, I slipped into the water and positioned myself behind the floating tub. The gates shut and I slowly maneuvered my barrel off into the distance.

At one point, I received a scare when two black guards came walking along the shore, loudly discussing whether or not they should take a shot at the tub. Fortunately, they did not, and I escaped without harm.

But safety remained a long way off. It took three painful weeks of slow and careful traveling before I found myself back within our lines. During that time, I worked my way along the northern bank of the Potomac, through the enemy capital, and back into Virginia. My gratitude to the kind, Southern families who gave me food, clothing and shelter cannot be expressed. Just as important was the timely arrival of Colonel Mosby's partisans at a moment when my recapture by Captain Mean's Loudoun Rangers seemed certain.

Allow me to relate just one incident which took place on the morning after my escape. I had spent the night most uncomfortably working my way along the coast and, somewhere near Leonardtown, I decided to chance the road. My bare feet suffered many bad cuts from rocks and shells, so progress was slow. I had already entered the roadway when I saw a Yankee soldier, sitting on a horse and holding a bottle of rum.

"Hello, Johnny. Where are you off to?" he asked.

"I'm goin' home, Yank," I stammered.

"Well, ain't you a lucky fellow? I wish I was going home, too."

Without another word, the Yank motioned with his bottle and allowed me to proceed. After that, I rarely traveled the roadway except at night.

Arriving in Richmond on August 15, which my diary noted as Napoleon's birthday, I eagerly applied at the War Department for the necessary papers to rejoin General Jackson, then commanding the Army of the Tennessee in Georgia. After much red tape, they granted me the travel documents.

The papers proved useless, however, for, on the morning I was due to depart, I fell ill, probably a result of the privations of prison life and prolonged exposure during my escape. Recuperating at my uncle's home in Richmond, I did not regain my health until late fall and could follow our army only through newspaper accounts.

Since Gettysburg, Jackson's fame continued to grow even as the fortunes of the Confederacy waned. In the fall of 1863, following the disaster at Missionary Ridge, he turned down Jefferson Davis' offer of command of the Army of the Tennessee; Joe Johnston was appointed, instead.

When the Army of the Potomac opened the 1864 spring campaign, Lee and Jackson successfully confronted the enemy in the Wilderness and Spotsylvania but were unable to prevent their sideways advances. When Lee became temporarily ill, Jackson took command and delivered a smashing blow to Grant's army on the North Anna. But even another defeat at Cold Harbor did not prevent Grant from continuing on toward Richmond. By early July, both armies were engaged in siege warfare around the Confederate capital and Petersburg to the south.

Meanwhile, in Georgia, "Retreating Joe" Johnston had been backed into the defenses of Atlanta by General Sherman's saucy Yankees; President Davis again asked Jackson to take command. While reluctant to do so in the midst of a campaign, it was obvious that, for the greater good of the cause, Jackson must accept leadership of the western army. In mid-July, he left the Army of Northern Virginia's earthworks around Petersburg and headed for the fortifications outside Atlanta.

Jackson opened by thoroughly thrashing the Yankee invaders on the banks of Peachtree Creek and a subsequent engagement east of the city brought a draw.

But the need to protect Atlanta frustrated Jackson's strategic genius and, consequently, there was no way to compensate for the overwhelming strength the enemy now mustered against the failing resources of the Confederacy. Had Jackson taken command when Sherman was still in the mountains of north Georgia, history would surely have seen a repeat of his 1862 Valley Campaign and the South would, today, be an independent nation. As it was, the two armies settled into a stalemate which lasted until November, when Sherman cut the final railroad into the city.

Freed from his tether, Jackson launched a magnificent campaign of maneuver which isolated the Yankees inside the city they had fought so hard to capture. Faced with a choice of retreat or moving toward Savannah, Sherman chose the latter. Jackson, outnumbered two-to-one, fought the Yankees to a draw in pitched battles near Covington, Milledgeville, and Macon, but Savannah fell on January 21, 1865. This was also General Jackson's 41st birthday.

During this same time, my physician reluctantly agreed that my condition had improved to the point that I could retake the field. I wrote and informed General Jackson of this and quickly received his taciturn reply: "Good. Come at once."

My first sight of General Jackson after so many months was a shock. Indeed, dear reader, I almost did not recognize him. He stood with several other officers, reviewing documents on a table in a farm house in South Carolina. He had lost weight, no doubt from a combination of scant rations, constant activity, and the anxiety of an increasingly difficult war. His brown hair, now streaked with gray, had thinned to near extinction on top. The lines were deeper on his face and he seemed older than his years, but the tired blue eyes still flashed with the unconquerable fire of battle.

Never talkative, he seemed quieter than ever, seldom breaking his silence except to comment on the military situation or to issue orders. When he did speak of other matters, his thoughts turned to his favorites who had been killed in the war. "Sandie" Pendleton, mortally wounded that fall, and J.E.B. Stuart, killed the previous spring, were often mentioned.

To the unbiased observer, it would have been obvious that the chance of success for our army had passed. Returning after so many months absence, I was shocked by the empty ranks and overall condition of our soldiers, but they bore their trials with little complaint.

Indeed, it seemed as if we had almost as many generals as private soldiers. Hardee, Johnston, Bragg, Hood and Beauregard were all there. But even this galaxy of stars could not affect the tide of battle this late in the war.

Following the fight at Bentonville, General Jackson gave temporary command of the army to General Johnston and, with me in tow, he journeyed to Petersburg for a conference with General Lee. For two days, March 31 and April 1, they discussed a plan to unite our armies and, in turn, defeat Sherman and then Grant.

The plan may have worked but the Yankees never gave us a chance to find out.

Before dawn, on Sunday, April 2, I rode to the house where General Jackson was staying with news that the enemy had captured part of our line near Rive's Salient. Jackson said nothing, but dressed quickly. Anna Jackson, holding their new-born infant, Virginia Stuart, escorted her husband to his horse and then watched from the window as we rode away. My mind recalled that day nearly two years before when the General and I had left Lexington.

We went to Lee's headquarters at Edge Hill, about a mile-and-a-half away. Lee's staff was astir, but the commanding general was not. Jackson entered Lee's chamber while I went off to hunt up something to eat. My search failed except for two small pieces of hardtack which came from a captured Federal haversack. I returned to find General Jackson mounted and about to leave.

"Come!" he shouted. "We are needed at the front."

We rode quickly toward the lines, passing some of our soldiers who warned us not to go farther. To emphasize the point, Yankee bullets began whistling past and we could see blue figures in the distance, near some of our winter huts.

Jackson did not hesitate but entered a body of woods where I feared Yankees might be waiting.

I summoned my courage and asked, "Excuse me, General, but where are we going?"

"Lieutenant, we must go over yonder and rally our line."

This took me aback for two reasons. First, I had never been addressed as "lieutenant" before and, second, I felt sure we would encounter the enemy riding in that direction.

We crossed the Boydton Plank Road and followed a wood line. We saw no one.

"Lieutenant, what day is today?"

" Sunday."

"Yes, it is Sunday and next week will be Palm Sunday. Wouldn't it be pleasant to go home and attend services in Lexington?" he asked softly.

We continued on and entered a field. Jackson scanned the horizon with his field glasses.

"There they are," he said, spying the enemy. "We'll go this way."

I held my revolver tightly and watched each tree for an ambush. Jackson raised his gloved hand and motioned me near.

"If anything should happen to me, go back and tell General Lee."

I nodded and we rode slowly ahead. It was a strange and suspended moment, less like a battlefield and more like a dream. The early morning light cast long shadows through the trees and, at any other time, thought may have turned to the coming spring. Now each breaking twig beneath our horses' hooves seemed to mark our passage toward an end which had already been decided.

Ahead we saw bluecoats in the woods. The two of them closest to us were, perhaps, twenty yards away and they ducked behind a tree for protection. Both lowered their rifles as if to aim.

"We'll take them," Jackson thundered, pulling his pistol and spurring his horse. I started to say, "No" but Jackson was gone. I hurried after him, my revolver cocked.

"Surrender!" Jackson yelled. "Our men are here."

"I can't see it!" a Yankee yelled back. "Let's shoot 'em!"

I urged my horse forward and tried to get in front of Jackson. Two shots rang out. One went wild, but the other hit its mark, striking Jackson's hand and continuing into his heart. Jackson reeled sharply, mouthed words I could not understand, and tumbled from the saddle. I fired blindly into the trees and then, leaning over the neck of my horse, made my escape. Jackson's riderless sorrel followed.[23]

Obeying instructions, I galloped back to army headquarters. General Lee, dressed in full uniform and saber, listened to my report. Tears welled up in his eyes and he seemed to sag visibly. Then, pulling himself back to his full height, he said softly, "General Jackson is at peace now. He has gone to a better place and we who are left are the ones to suffer."

Jackson's body was recovered by our men shortly thereafter. Placed in an ambulance, it arrived in Richmond only hours before the Northern Army entered the city. For several years, the body lay in Hollywood Cemetery, the grave marked only by a rough plank. Sometime after the war, a memorial committee was formed, chaired by Henry Kyd Douglas and myself. With Anna Jackson's blessing, we raised a public subscription to return the General to Lexing-

---

[23] Corporal John Mauck, of the 138th Pennsylvania Volunteer Infantry, fired the shot that killed Jackson.

ton and to erect an appropriate monument. That we accomplished in April 1875, the tenth anniversary of his death.

I accompanied General Ewell on the retreat to Appomattox and narrowly escaped capture at Saylor's Creek. I then joined up with General Gordon and took my parole following the army's surrender on April 9.

Returning to Lexington, I received, the little that remained of my father's estate and entered Washington College to complete my education. Once again, I came under the orders of Robert E. Lee, who honored that institution by serving as president until his death in October 1870.

Robert E. Lee standing at the grave of Stonewall Jackson in Lexington, Virginia. (Sergeant Kirkland's Museum and Historical Society)

Lt. General Thomas Jonathan Jackson (Courtesy of Massachusetts Commandery Military Order of the Loyal Legion and the US Army Military History Institute.)

EPILOGUE

CR   ഊ

Jefferson Carter Randolph had a difficult time adjusting to civilian life after the excitement of the war years. At Washington College, Randolph was an indifferent student who left the school before earning his degree.

For a time, he tried farming outside Lexington. Failing at that, he drifted down to New Orleans where he was employed by General James Longstreet at the Southern and Western Fire, Marine, and Accident Insurance Company. However, like Longstreet, Randolph got caught up in the post-war political strife of that city and left there after receiving threats from the White League.

With Longstreet's help, he secured a clerkship at the U.S. Patent Office and he remained in Washington, D.C., for nearly a decade. In 1877, he married Margaret Bee Bear of Alexandria, but the union was not a happy one. The couple separated after Margaret accidentally wounded Jefferson Randolph with a shot from his army revolver.

During his convalescence, Randolph began the first draft of his war memoirs but he, eventually, put the unfinished manuscript aside.

In the late 1880s, Randolph moved to San Francisco where he worked in a series of occupations before landing a position with the Southern Pacific Transportation Company. Here he became acquainted with Colonel John S. Mosby, the fabled partisan ranger. During the Spanish-American War, Randolph assisted Mosby in training a troop of light cavalry, although the force did not see action and never left the Bay Area.

Randolph also became friends with Ambrose Bierce, the famous writer and Hearst correspondent, and Bierce encouraged Randolph to finish the long-forgotten draft of his wartime experiences.

The manuscript was completed in 1913. However, it was never published because, that same year, Randolph accompanied Bierce to Mexico in order to see Pancho Villa's revolution firsthand. This last grand adventure ended badly as both men disappeared and were never heard from again.

In 1995, Randolph's original manuscript surfaced at the Tijuana flea market and this marks its first publication.

A SELECTED BIBLIOGRAPHY

Cℜ   ℬⅅ

Arnold, Thomas Jackson. *Early Life and Letters of General Thomas J. Jackson.* London and Edinburgh: Fleming H. Revell Co., 1916.

Battles and Leaders of the Civil War. Edison, NJ: Castle Books Edition. No date given.

Bean, William G. *The Liberty Hall Volunteers.* Charlottesville, VA: Univ. Press. of VA, 1964.

_____. *Stonewall Jackson's Man: Sandie Pendleton.* Chapel Hill, NC: Univ. of NC Press, 1959.

Benson, Berry. *Berry Benson's Civil War Book.* Athens, GA: University of Georgia Press, 1962.

Boatner III, Mark Mayo. *The Civil War Dictionary.* New York: David McKay Co., 1959.

Casler, John Overton. *Four Years in the Stonewall Brigade.* Guthrie, OK: State Capital Printing Co., 1893.

Catton, Bruce. *The Coming Fury.* New York, 1961.

Chambers, Lenoir. *Stonewall Jackson.* New York: W. Morrow, 1959.

Coddington, Edwin B. *The Gettysburg Campaign: A Study in Command.* New York: Charles Scribner's Sons, 1968.

Conrad, W. P., and Ted Alexander. *When War Passed This Way.* Greencastle, PA: White Mane Publishing, 1987.

Cook, Roy Bird. *The Family and Early Life of Stonewall Jackson,* Charleston, WV: Charleston Print. Co., 1948.

Dabney, Robert L. *Life and Campaigns of Lieutenant General Thomas J. Jackson.* New York: Blelock & Co., 1866.

Davis, Burke. *They Called Him Stonewall: A Life of Lt. General T. J. Jackson, C.S.A.* 1954. New York: Wings Books, 1988, Reprint.

Douglas, Henry Kyd. *I Rode With Stonewall.* Chapel Hill, NC: The Univ. of NC Press, 1940.

Farwell, Byron. *Stonewall: A Biography of General Thomas J. Jackson.* New York: W. W. Norton & Co., 1992.

Faust, Patricia L. *Historical Times Illustrated Encyclopedia of the Civil War.* New York: Harper & Row, 1986.

Frassanito, William A. *Gettysburg: A Journey in Time.* New York: Charles Scribner's Sons, 1975.

Freeman, Douglas Southall. *Lee*. Abridgment by Richard Harwell. New York: Collier Books, 1961

_____. *Lee's Lieutenants: Gettysburg to Appomattox*. New York: Charles Scribner's Sons, 1944.

Furgurson, Ernest B. *Chancellorsville, 1863: The Souls of the Brave*. New York: Vintage Books, 1992.

Gallagher, Gary W. *Stephen Dodson Ramseur, Lee's Gallant General*. Chapel Hill, NC: Univ. of NC Press, 1985.

Garrison, Webb. *Unusual Persons of the Civil War*. Fredericksburg, VA: Sergeant Kirkland's, 1996.

Hotchkiss, Jedediah. *Make Me a Map of the Valley: The Civil War Journal of Stonewall Jackson's Topographer*. Dallas: Southern Methodist University Press, 1973.

Klein, Frederic Shriver. *Just South of Gettysburg*. Westminster, MD: The Historical Society of Carroll County, 1963.

Longacre, Edward G. *The Cavalry at Gettysburg*. 1986. Lincoln, NE: Bison Book Edition, 1993.

Nye, Wilbur Sturtevant. *Here Come the Rebels!* 1965. Dayton, OH: Morningside Edition, 1984.

Robertson, James I. *The Stonewall Brigade*. Baton Rouge: Louisiana State Univ. Press, 1963.

Seagrave, Ronald R., *Civil War Books: Confederate and Union*. Fredericksburg, VA: Sergeant Kirkland's, 1997.

Tanner, Robert G. *Stonewall in the Valley*. New York, 1976.

Thomason, John William. *Jeb Stuart*. New York: Charles Scribner's Sons, 1930.

Tucker, Glenn. *High Tide at Gettysburg*. Dayton, OH: Morningside House Edition, 1973.

_____. *Lee and Longstreet at Gettysburg*. New York: Bobbs-Merrill, 1968.

Wert, Jeffry D. *General James Longstreet: The Confederacy's Most Controversial Soldier*. New York: Simon & Schuster, 1994.

Wyckoff, Mac. *A History of the 2nd South Carolina Infantry, 1861-1865*. Fredericksburg, VA: Sergeant Kirkland's, 1994.

_____. *A History of the 3rd South Carolina Infantry, 1861-1865*. Fredericksburg, VA: Sergeant Kirkland's, 1995.